Rabinowitz

1997

Knight on Horseback

ANN RABINOWITZ

Macmillan Publishing Company
New York
Collier Macmillan Publishers
London

Macmillan Publishing Company
866 Third Avenue, New York, NY 10022
Collier Macmillan Canada, Inc.
First Edition
Printed in the United States of America

10   9   8   7   6   5   4   3   2   1

The text of this book is set in 12 point Sabon.

Library of Congress Cataloging-in-Publication Data
Rabinowitz, Ann.
Knight on horseback.
Summary: Thirteen-year-old asthmatic Edward
reluctantly accompanies his family on a trip to
England, where he becomes acquainted with the ghost
of an historical figure, whose unclear intentions cause
Edward some anxiety before that relationship resolves
both itself and problems between Edward and his
father as well.
1. Richard III, King of England, 1452–1485—Juvenile
fiction. [1. Richard III, King of England, 1452–1485—
Fiction. 2. Ghosts—Fiction. 3. England—Fiction.
4. Fathers and sons—Fiction. 5. Asthma—Fiction]
I. Title.
PZ7.R1095Kn 1987   [Fic]   87-5520
ISBN 0-02-775660-2

*For my beloved family
without whose love and support
this would not have been written*

Knight on Horseback

I

Slowly, stealthily, Edward Newby eased the door to the hotel room shut behind him. Stiff with encrusted paint, the latch resisted. For agonizing moments he struggled with it. Suddenly it clicked to. In the hush the sound was shocking as a rifle shot. He froze, heart banging against his ribs. But along the hallway doors remained closed. No accusing voice rang out: *Eddy? Eddy Newby, where do you think you're going?*

At long last he expelled a breath and unclenched cramped fingers from the knob. His palms were slippery with sweat. Rubbing them against his jeans, he dared a cautious step. Then another. And another. Silent as a brave on the warpath he glided to the end of the hall and peered down into the stairwell.

Momentarily, by the dim light of the single fixture, he thought he glimpsed something—the barest flick of motion—on the landing below. Again he froze.

All the while that persistent voice in his head jeered: *Some adventurer! You're seeing things.*

Stung, he retorted: *Well, they oughta have more light. You could break your neck on those dumb steps. Serve 'em right if I did and my ghost came back to haunt them and . . .*

From the dining room two flights below, sounds and smells drifted up—a hum of conversation, the chink of cutlery on china, mouth-watering aromas of fresh-brewed coffee, toast and bacon. There was still time, plenty of time, to grab a bite and make a getaway before his family was up. Kate had been snoring when he sneaked out. From his parents' room had come no sound at all.

No! He wasn't going to risk it. Not today, with escape so close at hand. Though if his life depended on it, he couldn't have explained—not even to himself—just why he needed so badly to get away. He just knew he did. Because that trapped feeling had been growing on him since they had come to London. Since long before, in fact.

Escape! At the word excitement fizzed up in him like newly uncapped soda pop. He took the stairs two at a time and, ducking through the lobby to avoid the desk clerk's fishy stare, erupted out the swinging glass doors onto the London street.

The heat and roar of traffic struck like a blow. It was barely eight of a July morning, and already the day promised to be another scorcher. Sunlight hung heavy and stifling.

He stopped short. Where was he to go, all by himself in a strange city? Then he shrugged it off. What did it matter? He was free. Free after endless days of sightseeing, of trudging after his family through antique shops, museums and churches. Museums and churches! You'd think there was nothing else in London.

Light-headed with release, he capered along the street like a fugitive helium balloon. Over the lines between paving blocks he leapt high, sailing across to land smack in the middle of the next square. *Step on a crack, break your mother's back.* The words popped unbidden from the deeps of memory. Uneasy memory. Years ago his sister Kate had chanted them daily, walking him to kinder-

2

garten. Young as he was, he'd have died sooner than admit his terror at each misstep, or the overwhelming relief of finding his mother safe when he came home.

He slowed his pace. It was much too hot to run. He shoved a finger inside his collar and yanked the clammy fabric away from his neck. His clothes felt glued to him. How he longed for cool grass underfoot, or prickling his back as he lay in the shade of the maple in the yard at home. Though with his luck, he'd more likely be mowing the grass than lying in it!

Suddenly he grinned. What was he getting himself all worked up about? Home and chores were thousands of miles away across the ocean. And his family was still back at the stuffy old hotel. By now probably fussing over where he'd got to. He could almost hear them. His father would say, *Now, Margaret, you worry too much. Eddy can take care of himself. About time, too!* And from the lofty heights of sixteen years, Kate would put in her two cents: *After all, Mom, he's thirteen. No baby. Even if he acts like one.* While his mother—his mother would push the curls off her forehead with that nervous, birdlike gesture, protesting: *It's all very well for you to talk. But he doesn't know his way around London. And what if . . . what if he has an asthma attack?*

There it was! The word he hated. Tried never to use. Not even to himself. As if denying the disease a name would somehow cancel out the realities—panic, weakness, the desperate drowning struggle for breath.

Involuntarily his hand crept to his pocket, seeking out the bulge of spray bottle and pill container without which he went nowhere. Not even today. Not even in a bid for freedom.

He dragged his attention back to the problem at hand. Where was he to go? All his energies had been bent on jailbreak. He hadn't spared a thought for any sequel.

Regent's Park Zoo? Battersea Amusement Park? Place names surfaced, dredged from tedious hours over guide-books. His mother had been forever pressing them on him that past spring: *Where would you like to go, Eddy?* As if it made any difference what he wanted! He'd go wherever they took him. Like the luggage. You didn't ask your suitcase to choose, did you?

But zoos were for kids. And who wanted to go to an amusement park alone? You needed a friend. Someone to screech with when the roller coaster sent your stomach zooming right up through the top of your head.

The ominous roll of thunder cut short his meditations. Startled, he looked up into a darkening sky. Over the rooftops, fat black thunderheads were massing rank on rank. He quickened his step, but before he had gone a block further, raindrops splattered the hot pavements. By the time he reached the corner, the shower had turned into a deluge.

Placid beneath their ever-present black umbrellas, a group of Londoners stood queued up at the bus stop. As Eddy scurried past, a beefy woman grabbed his arm. " 'Ere, ducks, come under me brolly."

Any port in a storm. Besides, he had no choice. She outweighed him by at least a hundred pounds. He tried to squirm free, but she only took a fresh grip.

"Where's your mac?" she demanded.

"My what?"

"Your mac."

He stared.

She raised her voice. "Your mac. Macintosh. Rain-coat!"

"Oh . . . that. How was I to know it would rain?"

"Tourists," she sniffed. "It's a wonder you don't all catch your deaths." She fixed him with a suspicious look. "Your mum know you're out on your own? A little fellow like you . . ."

That did it! Always the shrimp of any crowd, he'd long since resigned himself to being last pick for the team, to still being let into movies at half price. But "little fellow" was too much. His temper rocketed toward blast-off.

Just then a bus hove into sight, a red double-decker lumbering like a hippopotamus through the downpour. His captor released him to fumble with the catch on her umbrella, and Eddy made good his second escape of the day. To his own surprise, and still with no clear goal in sight, he followed the woman onto the bus, then lurched up the swaying steps to the second level. As he hoped, her bulk discouraged her from following. A sudden stop catapulted him onto a seat, and he settled down to dry off and smooth his ruffled feathers.

Now, beyond the drowning windows, the great city of London unrolled itself for his inspection. Through the rain, the scenes took on the blurry softness of old photographs. He looked on dreamily, only half-aware that each and every muscle was uncoiling, relaxing like so many spent springs. Yet a knot remained in his stomach— excitement, an anticipation akin to the night before Christmas. Of what he didn't know.

The bus began to pass through shabbier neighborhoods. Here buildings huddled together, seemingly self-conscious over peeling paint and crumbled cornices. On

5

this wet and steamy morning few people were abroad; an occasional skinny cat scrounged among the garbage pails. Frayed lace strained to cover windows. In an upper story, a shade whisked up and was as hastily replaced.

Had a pallid face peered down? A small chill trickled along Eddy's spine; he hunkered down until they had passed by. For a moment he felt isolated, an unwelcome visitor to a scene as alien as a moonscape.

To his relief, he spied a small crowd gathered at the next corner. From below the conductor bawled: "Notting Hill Gate."

Impulsively, Eddy rose and dove for the steps. Moments later he was on the sidewalk and caught up in a noisy jostling throng. Unresisting, he allowed it to carry him along until at the next turning it swept left, to be absorbed into a larger hurly-burly.

He stopped dead in his tracks. Because nothing, nothing in those days of prickling boredom since they'd come could have prepared him for the scene before him.

Noises. Colors. Smells. People dressed in everything from rags to raincoats, flowing robes to blue jeans, bowler hats to turbans. White skins and black. Ivory. Yellow. Bronze. A cacophony of tongues. All swirling about as in some fantastic kaleidoscope, through the shops, stalls and stands that lined the road as far as the eye could see.

With a sigh of delight Eddy plunged into the melee. His blood was up. Visions of pirate treasure, of gold doubloons and pieces of eight danced before his eyes. Pushing and shoving, he elbowed his way to the nearest stand.

Some two blocks further and what seemed like hours later, bruised, buffeted, footsore and disillusioned, he pronounced judgment. "Junk!" he snorted, dismissing brasswares, cutglass, disco clothing, dusty books, antiques and a rack of used furs swaying in the breeze like so many scalp locks from a tepee ridge pole.

"Junk!" The kind his mother loved to paw through, haunting garage sales and antique shops—from which she was extricated only under protest.

"Junk!" he repeated for the third time, savoring the protest on his tongue. Or perhaps to distract himself from the creepy sensation centered right between his shoulder blades. As if someone or something were spying on him.

The rain had stopped. He started off again with renewed determination. Only to be brought up short. Was it his imagination, or had he caught the pad of furtive footsteps on his heels?

He whirled.

There was no one nearby. Unless you counted the organ grinder who stood cranking out tunes, a parrot perched precariously on his hat.

Idiot! Eddy scolded himself. *Dad's right for once. You've been reading too many horror stories. Watching too many scary movies on TV.*

He searched his pockets for a coin. As he leaned forward to drop it in the organ grinder's cup, the parrot spat a string of oaths at him. He jerked back, breath coming hard and fast.

Cold sweat stood out on his forehead and he must have paled, because a friendly voice inquired: "Anything wrong?"

He looked up. An elderly woman stood beside him. She was tall, so tall she had to crane her neck down to look into his face. With that long neck and worried frown, she reminded him of nothing so much as an anxious giraffe. He grinned.

An answering smile lit the blue eyes peering nearsightedly into his own. "I beg your pardon. I didn't mean to startle you. But you look a trifle seedy. Anything I can do?"

"No!" The denial was curt. As swiftly he regretted it. "I mean . . . no, thanks. The heat got to me, I guess. I'm okay now."

"Glad to hear it. It comes as a shock to visitors that London can be beastly hot in summer. They seem to expect rain and fog."

"That's how movies show it."

She nodded. "I suppose filmmakers think it adds atmosphere. And up north in Yorkshire, where I come from, it's all too true. We spend our lives half-frozen."

He brandished an inquiring hand. "What is this place? At home we've got garage sales and antique shops, but this . . ."

"It's a street market. Didn't you know? London's famous for them. This is Portobello Road. But if you hadn't heard, then how did you happen to come?"

"Oh, I kind of fell into it," he said with modest pride.

"Very enterprising of you! Now that you're here, how do you like it?"

He hesitated. Just too long.

She smiled. "A bit crowded and confusing?"

"Well . . ."

"I know. And full of awful junk at outrageous prices. Still, there are real treasures to be found, if one knows where to look. I come down twice a year to restock my shop."

8

She broke off and rummaged through her purse. "Now where . . . Ah!" She extricated steel-rimmed spectacles and clamped them to her nose. "That's better. I can see you properly. Now, where was I? Oh, yes. Street markets. Rather like the old medieval fairs, don't you think? Except not. Because those were real entertainment. Cockfights. Dancing bears. Magicians." Her face drooped, mourning lost glories. "Itinerant barbers and dentists. Lanced your boil with a dagger. Pulled your aching tooth with a pliers. For a fee, of course. And an audience."

He had a sudden vision of bright blood, flies, dust . . . the press of people. He shivered. She wagged a finger under his nose. "People weren't so squeamish in those days. Why, they sold ringside seats to public executions. Mothers would pack a picnic lunch and bring the brood. They say thousands turned out for the hanging of Dick Turpin, the famous highwayman."

Unexpectedly, a chuckle welled up in him. "Like the World Series."

"Or our World Cup football. Except no one made book on the outcome. Because the executioner always won. Ah, well, those days are gone forever. A good thing too. We're far more civilized now." But she looked none too happy about it.

"Well, young man, I must be getting along. Care to keep me company? You can tell me all about yourself."

To his astonishment he agreed. The words fairly tumbled out. "You see, my dad's a chemist. A research scientist. He's here to visit labs. And my mother's an English teacher. So she has to see all the literary places. Like where famous authors were born and . . ." He paused for breath. "And there's Kate, my sister. She thinks she's an artist. So she drags us to every gallery she can find. I didn't know there were so many pictures in the world."

She clucked sympathetically. "It doesn't sound very exciting for you. Isn't there something you'd especially like to see or do here?"

"No! I mean . . ." He blushed. "Well, I didn't want to come in the first place. My friend Pete asked me to go camping with him and his family, and—"

"Why didn't you?"

"My folks wouldn't let me. I guess they thought this was more educational or something."

She listened intently. Really listened. Come to think of it, she was the first grown-up he had ever met who listened. Mostly they just took possession of the conversation, turning and twisting it to secret purposes of their own.

She shook her head at last. "The trouble with you is, you're just like me. Living in the wrong day and age. No danger. No excitement. Nothing to get your teeth into. In the old days, you'd have been a man already. Working in the fields. Apprenticed to a craft. Or squire to some great knight. Married even." She smiled at his look of horror. "How old are you?"

"Thirteen."

"Well, perhaps not quite yet. Still, pity your poor parents. All unknowing, they've reared an eaglet in a robin's nest."

An eaglet in a robin's nest. He liked that. It sounded adventurous. Heroic. Nevertheless, he felt a pang of guilt. He hadn't so much as hinted at his asthma. The real reason—he was sure—why his parents hadn't let him go

10

camping. His mother worried. Sometimes the worry seemed to him to have a weight and mass all its own. Dragging him under.

"Why," the woman went on, "we're like as two peas in a pod. I'm sure we're destined to be fast friends." There seemed no need for further explanation. The current of sympathy flowed strong and sure between them.

Time flew. Soon they were laden with knobbly bundles—goods for the woman's shop, souvenirs and gifts for Eddy and his family and friends.

Yet through his pleasure, he was conscious of eyes on him. Staring eyes. Hungry eyes. He kept looking back over his shoulder. But he saw nothing.

Somewhere close-by a clock struck the hour. One . . . two . . . three. . . .

He exclaimed in dismay: "It can't be that late! My parents'll kill me!" Taking a fresh grip on his parcels, he said hastily, "It's been great. The best day ever. But if I don't show up soon, my mom will have them drag the Thames."

"I've loved every minute," she assured him. "Perhaps we'll meet again. Be sure to look me up when you come to Yorkshire. I'll drive you round to castles. Better still, I've a friend who owns a stables. He'll take you pony-trekking on the moor."

His face fell. "I don't know how to ride."

"It's never too late to learn. You've just the right build."

"I do?"

"Certainly. Haven't you ever gone to a horse race? Jockeys are all small and wiry. Not to speak of some of the world's greatest warriors—Richard the Third, Napoleon. . . . And what about Frodo the hobbit?"

"You've read Tolkien?" he said incredulously.

"*The Lord of the Rings* is a favorite of mine."

"I didn't know grown-ups read it. My dad says it's just a fairy tale."

"What's wrong with fairy tales? But don't get me started on that or we'll be here till midnight. And then what would your poor mother say?" Again she searched her pocketbook, dislodging a jumble of Kleenex, pencil stubs and other oddments in her eagerness.

She pressed a small cardboard oblong on him. "Here's my card. Don't lose it, because I'll be expecting you. Now I must fly."

He half expected her to do just that, rising into the air like Mary Poppins with her magic umbrella. He gazed forlornly after her until she was swallowed by the crowd. At last he glanced down at the card in his hand. CLAUDIA BOLTON, it read. ESTATES APPRAISED. ANTIQUES BOUGHT AND SOLD. MIDDLEHAM, YORKSHIRE. TEL: 035-4621.

About him the hubbub was dying down. Tired shoppers drifted homeward. Shopkeepers busied themselves packing away their wares for another week. An exhausted calm descended.

Reluctantly he turned back to the bus stop. How he hated to admit his great adventure was almost at an end! As he scuffed along, his eye was caught by the display in a shop window across the street. Even at this distance he could make out the gleam of metal, the sheen of burnished weaponry. Fatigue forgotten, he dashed between carts, almost bowling over several bystanders, to press his nose against the glass.

Under his entranced gaze lay the treasure trove of his

dreams: a collection of cutlasses, broadswords, dueling pistols, a murderously spiked mace. From deep in the shop's interior, a set of jousting armor brooded like some ancient sentinel over the hoard.

Odd. He hadn't noticed the shop before. But, with all the crowds and commotion, he supposed. . . . He pushed open the door and went in.

The light was dim, but he could not fail to see the dagger, displayed like a rare jewel against a square of crimson velvet. Scarcely daring to breathe, he moved forward, hands outstretched. Once some pirate captain had gripped this very blade. Once—

"Careful," a cool voice cautioned. "It's razor-sharp. Best not to touch."

He snatched his hand back. "I only wanted to look."

"Of course." Then as Eddy turned away, the man caught at his arm. "Here, son. Don't run off. I can see you meant no harm. It's only that on market day one can't be too careful. Look here." He took a wooden object from the shelf behind him and blew on it to dislodge a coating of dust.

Reluctantly, Eddy obeyed. But as his hand closed over the dark wood, he suppressed an exclamation. Something very like an electric shock tingled up his arm.

Now by the gray light slanting through the windows, he saw he held a statue of a knight on horseback. It was small, no more than five or six inches high. Yet so real was it that under his questing fingers, hot blood seemed to course the charger's hide. Sharp hooves fled away; mane and tail were borne out on some clean, invisible wind. The rider sat his mount in pride and courage. One mailed fist gripped the reins; the other brandished high a mighty broadsword. Already the weapon was battle-tested, its tip severed in a jagged break.

Eddy drew a long, shaky breath. Before his eyes the market swam crazily. People, stands, the store in which he stood were growing indistinct. At last they vanished altogether.

Through every fiber in his body he felt the piston pumping of his charger's stride. He tightened steel-encased thighs about the lathered flanks; his mount responded with a burst of speed. As they thundered across the fields, the crushed grass underfoot gave up its scent—pungent, almost unbearably sweet.

All about him men and horses plunged on. The din was so great he could distinguish no single sound, but his own throat was hoarse with shouting. Inside the battle helm sweat ran down, furrowing his dusty cheeks. His eyes stung with it. He could see the enemy framed in his visor slot—a line of rigid metal figures waiting, weapons ready. Overhead, the whine of arrows signaled that the archers were about their deadly work.

A figure loomed up, a black knight mounted on a great black horse. His poised sword glittered in the sunlight. Yet Eddy felt no fear, only exultation. He raised his own sword. . . .

"Beautiful piece of work, isn't it? Though hardly museum quality with that broken sword. I could let you have it cheap."

"What?" How strange his own voice sounded. Was it the helmet?

"I said—" In the recesses of the store a phone shrilled.

14

The proprietor uttered an exclamation of annoyance. "I shan't be a minute."

A splatter of drops against the glass heralded fresh rain. Thunder prowled the sultry skies again.

The street door opened and a man stood there. Lightning streaked behind him, etching him with livid clarity against the air. Eddy caught his breath. For one moment he thought the man deformed, an armless monster. Then, with a tremor of relief, he saw that he was only wrapped from neck to knee in a long, dark cloak.

Yet he took a step back. The face before him was not reassuring. Pale and expressionless, it was framed in long dark hair that hung lank with moisture. The forehead was broad, creased above the nose by a tiny fan of frown lines. Thin lips clamped into a slash, as if determined to give nothing away.

The silence deepened. Eddy tried to look away. But the eyes held his. In the storm light, they glowed tawny as dead amber petrified long aeons past. He could see himself reflected there, a tiny fly forever caught.

He cleared his throat. "Should I buy this?" Even as he spoke he wondered what had made him say it. Whatever the price, it would be too expensive. Yet he had had to say something. Anything to break the silence. There was something else too. Something he couldn't put his finger on. But the man looked familiar. As if he'd seen him before. Somewhere. Sometime.

The man made no response. Just went on staring.

Eddy panicked. Scarcely conscious of what he did, he fled into the street. Not until he rounded the first corner did he remember that he still clutched the little statue.

Sanity returned with a rush of scorching shame. What had he done? A summer storm, a chance encounter and, as usual, his overactive imagination had run away with him. He stood convicted. Not just of cowardice, but shoplifting. He was a thief!

There was nothing to do but go back. Back to brave the cloaked man. Back to explain—as best he could—to the suspicious shopkeeper. Had he called the police yet? What would his parents say—or do—when they found he'd been arrested?

He forced himself to turn, to set one reluctant foot before the other. The thunderclap that followed was so loud he was sure the city would crumble under its fury. He shrank back. At that instant he caught sight of the cloaked man coming after him.

Casting resolution to the winds, he took to his heels. Fear lent him speed. At first he seemed to gain on his pursuer. But it was an unequal contest. He could not match that ground-devouring stride for long. Soon, all too soon, the cloaked man drew abreast of him.

Gasping, Eddy stopped and leaned against a railing, fighting for breath. His chest felt squeezed in an iron vise. With shaking hands, he dragged the spray from his pocket and squirted it into his nose and mouth.

The cloaked man was not two feet away, but Eddy was too absorbed in keeping his head above the drowning tide to care. Through the drumming in his ears, over the rasps that tore his chest, he heard the man exclaim: "You are not well, lad!"

"Be okay . . . in a sec . . ."

"You have taken a chill." The voice was gentler, but

rusty. Like an unused gate. Was this how junkies sounded? Crazies?

"Show me the statue!"

Startled, Eddy looked up. The face was only inches from his.

He obeyed. Better this way, after all. The man would take it back. Meanwhile, he could make his getaway.

But to his astonishment the other made no effort to touch the statue, only devoured it with his eyes. He sighed. "It is as I thought."

Down the street Eddy could see a bus approaching, headlights glinting in the gloom. He poised for flight.

"Farewell, Edward."

"You know my name?"

Something flickered across the rigid features. The harsh voice shook. "How should I have forgotten?"

Brakes squealing, the bus swung in to the curb. Incredulous at this easy escape, Eddy climbed aboard. Not till they were under way did he venture to look back.

The rain-swept corner was deserted. The man had gone.

II

The sky was clearing and a late sun edged still-heavy clouds with gold as Eddy trudged the last blocks back to the hotel. His empty stomach growled, his feet ached, and with each step the packages grew heavier.

But somewhere on the long ride back, guilt had given way to resignation. What was done was done. So far, at least, there was no sign of pursuit.

Even so he'd spent the better part of the bus trip camouflaging the statue with tag ends of paper from the other parcels. Somehow, someway, he would find the means to return it undetected. Until then no one must be the wiser.

Meanwhile, if not happy he was at peace. He had set forth that morning like some knight of the Round Table on the high quest for adventure. Success had crowned his efforts. He returned home booty laden.

Far up the street he saw his mother standing on the hotel steps, anxiously scanning the passersby. When she caught sight of him she waved, relief in every line of her body.

He maintained his unhurried pace, acknowledging her greeting with a nod. The salute set the plumes on his helmet to waving; they sketched a scarlet arc against the air. At the foot of the steps he dismounted, tossing the reins to a waiting squire.

Mrs. Newby threw her arms about his neck. "Where have you been? I was so worried! I thought—"

18

Bitterly he wondered if Marco Polo had endured a similar greeting on his return from twelve long years in far Cathay.

"Why, you're wet through!" she exclaimed. "Oh, Eddy! You know how easily you catch cold. And then your asthma flares up and— Why didn't you take your raincoat?"

"My mac," he corrected.

"What?"

His father appeared in the doorway behind her. His eyes met Eddy's. The look was disapproving, and Eddy flinched. "Where have you been? You might at least have let us know. It's teatime already. Go get cleaned up and meet us in the dining room."

None too gently he steered Eddy through the lobby and toward the stairs. In his room, Eddy tossed the parcels onto the bed and headed for the bathroom. His exhilaration had drained away, leaving him flat and defeated.

Halfway across the room he swung about in dismay. How could he have forgotten? Kate might come in at any minute. Hastily he retrieved the statue and stuffed it into his suitcase. Not till the case was stowed at the back of the closet did he let himself relax.

Kate had obviously just vacated the bathroom; the air was steamy with perfumed bath oil. Sink and shelf alike were littered with cosmetics. He wrinkled his nose. How could she stand that junk?

Glimpsing himself in the mirror, he leaned forward, scrubbing at the misted surface. Try as he would, there was no quelling a momentary surge of hope.

But hope for what? A different image? If so, he was

19

doomed to disappointment. The same old Eddy stared sullenly back at him—skinny, undersized. Half-baked, he thought suddenly. That's me. Half-baked. Baby-fine brown hair hung limp about his small pale face. Gray eyes were underscored with bluish circles. From each nostril a pinched line ran diagonally down to the corners of the mouth. Lines carved there by the frequent struggle for breath.

Feeling obscurely betrayed, he backed away and turned the taps on in the tub. When it was full, he stripped and stepped in. For some time he lay motionless, a half-submerged hulk hull down in a placid sea.

A rude banging at the door roused him finally.

"For Pete's sake, Eddy! What are you doing? We're starved."

"Keep your shirt on. I'm taking a bath."

"Now?" she squawked. "There won't be any food left by the time we get there."

"Dad said to clean up."

Deliberately he arched his back so he could pee up into the air. The stream shot clear across the room and splattered the tile of the far wall. He sank back, satisfied he had set a distance record.

The doorknob turned. He leapt from the tub, grabbing for a towel. But only Kate's hand appeared. It deposited a heap of clothing and withdrew. He heard a giggle, then the sound of retreating footsteps.

Fuming, he bent to pick up the clothes. Why couldn't they just let him alone? *Wear your raincoat. Don't catch cold.* As if he got sick on purpose. *Get cleaned up. Hurry. Hurry. Hurry.* The litany of complaint was soothing. As

20

he reached down to pull up his jockeys, something caught his eye. He stood transfixed, examining himself. Sure enough, a few faint wisps of hair showed on his groin. He let out a whoop. "Fuzz!"

Good humor restored, he ran to join the others. His spirits rose still further when he saw the table. Kate's prophecy of famine had been premature. There were platters of sandwiches and relays of toast. There were preserves; his greedy glance identified strawberry, currant and marmalade. There was cream so thick it looked like butter. There was cake in thick slabs that overflowed the plate. Crowning the feast was the teapot, as round and brown and fat as any beehive.

John Newby was the first to admit defeat. Pushing his chair back with a groan, he extended long legs and dug through his pockets for a pipe. Soon, a fragrant blue-gray haze spiraled ceilingwards.

Unlooked for and so doubly poignant, a vision of their kitchen at home rose before Eddy's eyes: walls hung with utensils, a jungle of plants on every sill, the old dog Merlin whining in sleep on his rug. He could hear him clearly. He whispered: "Merlin?" Only to shake his head in disgust. Because, of course, Merlin wasn't here but in the boarding kennel at home. Would he be all right till they got back? He'd looked so lonely when they left him. Even Dr. Newby had said, "I feel like a murderer."

Eddy shoved his plate aside. It skidded across the starched cloth like a surfboard to collide with the toast rack. The clatter rose sharply over the hum of talk.

At nearby tables heads swiveled round, then politely turned away again. His parents frowned.

Let them look! He didn't care. It felt so good to let the discontent boil over. Better, anyway, than to admit to the wave of homesickness that had swept over him.

His mother sighed. "I wish you'd come with us instead of running off like that. We went to the Victoria and Albert Museum and St. Paul's Cathedral and—"

Museums and churches. He made a rude sound in his throat.

"Well, every English teacher dreams of seeing them. The names alone are sirens to this old fire horse." The tone was light but her eyes were wistful.

Suddenly he felt small and mean for having spoiled her pleasure.

"Oh, Mom, I'm sorry but . . ." But what? What was the matter with him? Lately he was forever spoiling for a fight, exploding into words he didn't mean and regretted the moment they were spoken. Then came remorse, resolutions not to be so touchy. Until not ten minutes later the black tide would rise again in his chest.

"Tell us about your day," his father said. "What did you do?" The words challenged.

Before, you didn't have time to listen, Eddy thought. Now, just because I was rude to Mom . . .

Once launched, however, he held forth like an explorer. Just talking about it brought the market back to him—its sights, sounds and smells, the exotic throng of people surging through the streets.

Not till he came to Claudia Bolton did he falter. He knew all too well what his father would make of an adult who loved Tolkien. And he could just imagine what his mother would think of someone who joked about public executions. One of his earliest memories was of his mom pushing him in his stroller at a rally against capital punishment, a weary Kate whining at their heels.

He contented himself with a lame "She was nice." Nice! What kind of word was that to describe the funniest, most interesting friend he'd ever made?

He started over. "She was tall and skinny. Kind of like a giraffe." Kate giggled, and he crimsoned. Some friend he was! Betraying the woman for a cheap laugh.

"She . . . uh . . . invited me, I mean us, to visit her in Yorkshire. We're going there, aren't we?"

His mother nodded absently.

Inspiration came to him. "She has an antique shop."

His mother brightened. "Sounds delightful. I'd love to meet her."

Perversely, jealousy stabbed. Did he really want to share her? She was his friend. The first adult one he had ever had. Not counting relatives and teachers. And you couldn't really call them friends.

Later, he blundered onto treacherous ground. "I found a store that sold armor and swords and . . ." The words died away.

To cover his confusion, he reached for the cake plate. Only to watch helplessly as tea flowed from an overturned cup into Kate's lap.

"Pig!" she hissed. "Just look at my skirt. Mother, you've just got to teach him some manners. He's nothing but a"—she spluttered, searching for an epithet—"a pint-size barbarian!"

"Even barbarians have to eat," he retorted. "Except the fat ones, of course. Like you."

Bull's eye! Kate turned scarlet. Every freckle blazed as she stuck out her chin, squared sturdy shoulders and seemed ready to abandon her hard-won dignity in a brawl.

Dr. Newby cut in. "Enough! Eddy, apologize to your sister."

"What for?" he muttered. But his father had heard. His lips tightened ominously and Eddy capitulated. "I'm sorry," he mumbled.

To his exasperation, his mother looked on the verge of tears. She dabbed at Kate's skirt with a napkin.

Eddy stared morosely at his father, wishing for the zillionth time that he'd inherited his build instead of his mother's slight frame. John Newby topped six feet four and was as broad as any halfback. Though years hunched over desk and laboratory bench had given him a perpetual slight stoop. But if the build was that of a football player, the face was a scholar's—serious, lined, topped by an untidy shock of pepper-and-salt hair.

With a start, Eddy found his father staring back at him. The narrow blue eyes—Viking eyes, his wife called them, conjuring up images of those fierce warriors braving the salt spray—seemed to bore into Eddy's brain. He squirmed. Lucky there was no such thing as a mind reader. So long as he kept his cool his secret would be safe. Except from the cloaked man. And he was back at the market. Or wherever he hung out. Unless . . . could he have followed him?

He stood up. "I'm going back to the room. To read. Mess around."

It was all he could do not to run. By the time he got upstairs his hands were shaking so he could barely unlock the suitcase. He heaved a sigh of relief. The bundle was as he had left it. The voice said mockingly, *What did you think? The old geezer flew in the window like Superman and took it?*

He paid no attention. But the urge to see and touch the statue once again was overpowering. He tore back a corner of the paper, exposing bare wood. Tentatively he stroked it. Again that odd shock of electricity ran up his arm.

Mysteriously, there was no need to examine further. Knight and horse were clear in his mind's eye. As familiar as the teddy bear he had so recently banished from his bed. Each plane, each curve, each detail seemed imprinted on his brain.

Later he tossed and turned in his hot bed, unable to sleep. Passing headlights in the street below cast quicksilver reflections on the wall. They only mirrored the confusion of his thoughts.

Why had he taken the statue? Had it really been a mistake? Or had he meant to all along? And where had he seen the cloaked man before? Had he been following Eddy all day, eyes fixed on his prey through the stolen hours of freedom? Would Eddy ever see him again?

Morning dawned as stifling as ever. Even his mother seemed jaded, though she rallied her flock briskly to tour the Houses of Parliament.

By noon Dr. Newby put his foot down. "Enough!" he said firmly. "Let's take a boat upriver to the Tower. It'll be cooler on the water. And from there we'll go by Underground to Madame Tussaud's Wax Museum." Catching Eddy's eye he winked. "Right up your alley, son. Plenty of blood and gore."

The river proved a welcome relief. Cat's-paws ruffled the murky waters and played across the decks of the boat.

Dr. and Mrs. Newby sank down onto a bench in the shade, and Kate retired to the stern with sketch pad and pencil. Eddy made his way forward and leaned over the bow rail, munching a muffin he had stowed away from breakfast.

If this were a movie, he thought, a body would float by now. All slimy and bloated and . . . He peered into the water. Under his fascinated gaze, a face materialized. Dead eyes stared up sightlessly, tawny eyes set in a face of leaden pallor. About it the hair fanned out like seaweed, rippling limply on the current.

Hastily he shut his eyes. When he dared look again the face was gone.

Disembarking passengers were met at Tower Wharf by a Yeoman Warder, member of the famous guard. Smartly turned out in scarlet flannel, starched neck ruff and broad black hat, he might have stepped straight out of one of those old portraits Kate made such a fuss over.

He set a brisk pace as he led the tourists into the grounds of the ancient fortress. His ruddy face glowed, his smile broadened as he recounted tale after tale of plots, betrayals, torture and beheadings.

"Look there!" He pointed to a squat square structure. "That's the famous 'Bloody Tower.' Where the little princes died. No doubt you've heard of 'em. Their wicked uncle Richard had them suffocated so's he could take the throne." He pulled his face into suitably grave lines. "Lambs for the slaughter, that's wot I calls 'em. Lambs for the slaughter," he repeated, with evident enjoyment. "Now, then! Step lively and we'll take a dekko at the spot."

Fairly galloping ahead, he led his charges inside and up

26

a corkscrew stair cut deep into the wall. At the summit they huddled in the gloom to peer into a tiny chamber.

"That's it!" the guide announced, proud as if he'd brought them safe up Everest. "The princes' chamber. Went to bed one night and never come out again. Never seen again by mortal man."

Behind him, Eddy heard Kate draw breath. He squeaked as her fingers dug into his shoulders.

The tour continued in the same vein, through armories and torture chambers, and past the Crown Jewels. It reached its climax on Tower Green, where the Warder pointed out the spot where highborn prisoners had fallen to the headsman's ax.

"What a ham!" Margaret Newby snapped as the guide exited to a round of applause. "Come on. We'd better be on our way."

Heels tapping on the cobbles she made for the gate. Kate and Dr. Newby followed, two liners towed by an energetic tug.

Eddy trailed after them. How he wished Mrs. Bolton had been there. She, at least, would have appreciated the Warder's talk.

The Wax Museum was disappointing at first. In its stuffy halls, replicas of the famous and the infamous alike rubbed shoulders—Admiral Nelson, Henry the Eighth with his gaggle of wives, Queen Elizabeth and Prince Philip, John Kennedy and Richard Nixon. Eddy lost count. And interest. There were so many.

Yet as time passed, he grew uneasy. There was something spooky about those painted figures with their high color and staring eyes. Eyes that followed you everywhere.

And down in the basement, lit in what Eddy privately dubbed "gruesome green," was the Chamber of Horrors. Here Jack the Ripper stalked the London fog again in search of victims. And a bespectacled Christie kept watch over a cupboard full of murdered women. There was Mrs. Dyer, strangler of forty-six babies. And an early ecologist—Eddy never learned his name—who disposed of victims in vats of acid.

"Less left to litter," Eddy quipped. But he felt queasy. As if he'd eaten too much ice cream. He longed for fresh air.

"Now for the tableaux," his mother announced.

Kate set up a wail. "Oh, Mom, my feet hurt. Let's go back to the hotel."

"They're the most educational exhibits. Historical scenes, like Guy Fawkes and the Gunpowder Plot, and the execution of Mary, Queen of Scots, and —"

Dr. Newby sighed. In the greenish light he looked drawn. "All right, Margaret. Come on, kids. Or we'll never hear the end of it."

Eddy shuffled along as slowly as he dared, eyes rebelliously on the floor. But Kate's whisper penetrated his indifference.

"C'mere, Eddy!"

Reluctantly he crossed the hall. Before them was a scene of an old-fashioned bedchamber, where two boys slept in a curtained bed. The older lay on his back, face flushed and peaceful in sleep. The younger cuddled close, head buried in his brother's shoulder, an arm flung carelessly across his chest.

Eddy recoiled. It wasn't fair to stare at them! He hated

to be spied on when he was asleep. Sometimes when he was sick, his mother would creep into the room at night to check on him. It made him feel exposed. Naked, even. Did she think he'd died?

Kate started to say something. He turned on her, a warning finger to his lips.

She smiled. "I know. They're so real you think you'll wake them."

Danger stalked the sleeping pair. Two men hovered close. One stood with his back to the hall, guarding against attempted rescue. The other leaned forward, a pillow clasped in his hands. The menace was unmistakable. Any second the man would pounce, bring down that smothering weight on the boys' heads!

A shout rose in Eddy's throat, only to die away again. Useless to protest. These were only dolls, wax puppets forever caught up in some grotesque game of freeze-tag. The real crime had been committed hundreds of years before.

"The little princes," Mrs. Newby murmured.

Kate said fiercely, "Why were they killed?"

"Didn't you listen to the Warder? Their uncle wanted the throne. They stood in his way, so he had them shut up in the Tower and murdered."

Kate shuddered. "The poor kids!"

"It makes you feel so helpless," said Dr. Newby. "Not being able to do anything."

His wife said nothing. For a moment more she stood still, then with a tiny shrug she turned away. Kate and Dr. Newby followed. Eddy gripped the velvet guard rope, as if defying them to tear him away. A short while before he had longed to leave. Now something deep inside compelled him to stand and watch. As if by the intensity of his look he might penetrate some dark secret.

The bedclothes clung. The boys' heartbeats, so close they could have been his own, thundered through his body. Something—some breath or movement—warned him of impending danger. His eyes flew open. The pillow was descending. In the face behind it he could read no pity. Only death! He tried to scream; even as his mouth opened, the pillow was upon him. He kicked and struggled, flailing wildly.

It was the voice in his head that saved him. *You're nuts! Loony, that's what. Come on. Let's get outta here. Come on!*

To get away. Yes, that was it. He had to get away before he was sucked under. Forever!

He looked wildly about. As he did so, the hall steadied. His frenzied gasps eased. In the tableau, murderers and princes remained fixed in their fatal moment.

Suddenly Eddy leaned forward, straining to pierce the gloom. There was a third man in the scene, half-hidden by the draperies behind the bed. Funny. He hadn't seen him before.

The man's face was shadowed, hardly more than a pale blur. Dark hair hung to his shoulders, grazing the cloth of his . . . Was it a jacket? A coat? A . . . cloak?

Eddy's heart began to pound. It was just another wax figure. It had to be. But if so, why hadn't he noticed him before? And why did the cloth across his breast move— gently but surely to the rise and fall of breath?

He stood rooted. Like a rabbit petrified before a snake,

30

waiting for the tawny eyes to turn on him. At last he began to back away. Slowly at first. Then faster. And still faster. Until he was running full tilt down the hall. Past Guy Fawkes in the grip of soldiers. Past Mary Stuart kneeling to her executioners. The tableaux blurred.

He caught up with the others at the street exit. As they walked slowly toward the Underground, he pressed close.

Kate shoved at him. "Uncrowd, Eddy. It's too hot." Then she looked more closely at him and her face changed. "What's the matter? Don't you feel well?"

"Back there . . ."

"Creepy, wasn't it? All those eyes."

"No. I meant that one scene." He couldn't bring himself to name it.

"Which?" she teased.

"You know."

"Oh, that. The princes. That was gross. I thought I'd be sick. C'n you imagine waking up with a pillow over your face?"

He could. Only too well. He said hastily, "D'ya notice the guy . . ."

"Who? The guard or the man with the pillow?"

"Neither. The man at the back. Behind the curtains."

She smiled. "Wouldn't you adore a bed with curtains like that? When I get married . . ."

"Oh, for chrissakes, Kate!"

His mother whirled. "That's enough, young man! I don't want to hear you talk like that. Understand?"

"Sorry," Kate whispered. "I got you into that. What were you talking about?"

"The third man."

"I don't know what you mean. There were only two. Aside from the kids."

"But—"

His mother broke in. "It just goes to show how too much imagination and an overdose of horrors can do you in. I blame myself. I never should have let you come to the Wax Museum after listening to the Warder. You know, when I was little I couldn't sleep for months worrying about a bear hidden in my closet, waiting to jump out and eat me."

"Didn't your parents tell you it was just your imagination?" Kate asked.

"Oh, I wouldn't have dreamt of going to them. For fear they'd laugh at me."

They walked on in silence. As they went down into the Underground, Kate said, "The light wasn't so good back there. Maybe it was just an optical illusion. Or maybe one of the guards was playing a practical joke. Like the policeman on the stairs everyone thought was wax until he moved. Remember, Eddy?"

An optical illusion? A practical joke? He didn't know. He only knew he was glad the day was over. Glad, for once, of his family close beside him.

III

The heat broke their last night in London, exploding into tantrums of thunder that set windows to rattling in their frames and torrents of rain sluicing down sun-baked gutters.

Waiting on the hotel steps the next morning for delivery of their rental car, Eddy shivered in the chill.

"Put your sweater on," Kate ordered. "Or you'll get sick and ruin the trip. You're all over goose bumps."

He ignored her. "There it is!"

"It can't be," said John Newby at his shoulder. "I asked for something bigger."

But the little car pulled in at the curb. The driver climbed out.

"Isn't it adorable?" said Kate.

Eddy had to admit it was cute. Resplendent with scarlet paint and glittering chrome, it looked like a giant's toy magically set down on the London street.

Only Dr. Newby seemed less than enchanted. He circled the little car twice, examining each detail and prodding all four tires with a suspicious toe before he climbed in. Maneuvering his large frame behind the wheel required effort; he had to double over and slide in crabwise. Once seated, he could be seen wrestling with seat adjustment and window cranks. But at last the glass rolled down and his flushed face appeared in the aperture.

"I reserved a station wagon, not a kiddy car," he said through tight lips. "Haven't you anything bigger?"

The driver looked crestfallen. "It's our busiest season and a number of cars haven't been returned on schedule. If you could wait a few days . . ."

"Impossible! We're due in Warwick tonight, we have tickets for the Shakespeare theater in Stratford for tomorrow and I must be in Nottingham on business at the end of the week."

He extricated himself panting, unable to uncoil to full height until he was on the sidewalk again. "Give me the keys and papers," he snapped. "We'll have to make do."

"You could slide the sunroof back and ride with your head out," Kate suggested.

Eddy snickered, but their father reddened. He opened his mouth to reply, then shut it again.

The driver said hastily, "I'm sure you'll find it satisfactory. Good things come in small packages, I always say." He patted his charge lovingly on its metallic flank and, evidently reluctant to surrender it, added, "Shall we take her out for a quick spin, sir? Driving on the left takes some getting used to. And if you've a map, I'll mark out the route to Warwick."

Eddy and Kate exchanged looks. Never in memory had their father admitted to a need for directions. He had been known to circle for an hour or more like a bloodhound off the scent, rather than stop and ask.

Just then the bellhop staggered down the steps under a mountain of luggage. Mrs. Newby followed closely. When she saw the car, she stopped and frowned.

"Is that it?"

Her husband nodded grimly.

We'll never get everything in."

"We might have. If you and Kate hadn't brought every outfit you own and bought out half of London too."

It took brute force to wrestle the luggage into the tiny trunk. Mrs. Newby alternately exhorted and advised. Kate repeated over and over like a stuck cuckoo clock, "It won't fit . . . won't fit . . . won't fit. . . ." The bellhop hovered. The rental car driver beat a prudent retreat.

To everyone's amazement the cantankerous mass surrendered at last. Quick as lightning, Dr. Newby slammed the lid down and locked it. Stray parcels were lashed to the roof, and the passengers climbed in. They swung smoothly out into traffic.

"I can't for the life of me see why everyone makes such a fuss about driving on the left side of the road," said Dr. Newby. "It takes good reflexes, but for an old tank driver like me . . ." He flashed a triumphant grin at his wife.

Eddy gritted his teeth. Sometimes he thought he hated his father in this know-it-all mood. The worst of it was, he so often turned out to be right.

"Please, dear," Margaret Newby begged, "keep your eyes on the road."

They swooped around the corner. Mrs. Newby screamed. Kate moaned and covered her eyes.

"Look out!" Eddy shouted.

Brakes squealed. They jerked to a stop, head to head with a massive bus. Dr. Newby's reflexes had directed him unerringly back to the righthand side of the road.

Traffic ground to a halt. A prickly silence fell in the car as Dr. Newby backed and filled, extricating them from the knot of stalled vehicles. Eddy stared at the floor, avoiding the smiles of passersby.

An uncomfortable half hour passed. At last they pulled into a quiet side street and stopped. Dr. Newby mopped his face. "Sorry. I had no idea. You have to unlearn everything." He got out a map and spread it over the dashboard.

"Let's see now. I'll pick up the highway here and . . . yes, that takes us straight into Oxford."

"O-Oxford!" A long-conquered stammer still plagued Mrs. Newby in moments of excitement. "I had no idea you planned . . ."

She turned to the backseat. "Just think, children. One of the oldest universities in the Western world!"

"Big deal," Eddy muttered. But he took care she didn't hear.

His parents were smiling at each other. They looked as pleased as if they'd inherited the Crown Jewels, he thought. He felt forlorn, excluded from their happy secret.

Soon they had left city and suburbs behind. The air was soft and cool, the grass of the highway verges a brilliant emerald. A light rain began to fall.

Dr. Newby switched on the windshield wipers. "Good old England."

"We've been lucky so far," said his wife defensively. "I haven't used my umbrella at all."

All anyone in England talked about was weather, Eddy thought. In London every second sentence had been "How hot it is!" Or "Isn't it beastly?" He closed his eyes.

The blare of car horns woke him. "Where are we?"

"Oxford," said his mother.

Dr. Newby had to raise his voice to be heard over the motorcycle engine revving up beside them. "Keep a sharp eye out for a parking space."

It was tantalizing. They caught fleeting glimpses of the fabled spires and buildings as they passed. Mrs. Newby tolled off landmark names—eagerly at first, then with increasing wistfulness. Because nowhere, nowhere in the crush of cars, buses, lorries, bicycles and scurrying pedestrians was there a space to be found.

At last she sighed. "I give up. Let's find a supermarket and buy sandwich makings. We can picnic by the roadside on the way to Warwick." She shook her head mournfully. "I haven't even seen an academic gown. They wear them year-round here, you know."

"Sounds dumb to me," said Kate. Privately, Eddy agreed.

He insisted on staying in the car while the others shopped. He knew what it would be like. His mother would argue for roast beef, while Dr. Newby pleaded for sardines. Yukk!

Claudia Bolton's words came back to him. She had said a boy his age would have been *squire to some great knight*. What would he have eaten and drunk in those days? Game, maybe. Beer or wine. Would he have had his own horse? A sword?

Down the street he heard a door slam. Idly he turned to watch as a man emerged from a row house and walked toward the car. He was somberly dressed. The breeze set the folds of his dark garment to billowing behind him.

Eddy smiled and reached for the door handle. Maybe he could find his mother. One of her wishes, at least, would come true. She would see an academic gown.

Then he stiffened and his hand dropped back to his side. The man was too far off to see his face. But surely the stride was familiar. And was that really an academic gown, or was it a long dark cloak?

Eddy shut his eyes tightly and slid down on the seat, wishing himself invisible.

The car door opened and he started violently. A hand fell on his shoulder.

"Hey!" said Kate. "It's only me. Hope you're hungry. We bought out the store."

He steeled himself and looked up and down the street. It was empty.

Beyond Oxford they turned off the highway into a maze of country lanes. Along both sides of the road, hedgerows were fragrant with honeysuckle and dog-rose. Meadow flowers stood tall in the fields beyond.

"Real English countryside," Mrs. Newby murmured. "'I sing of brooks, blossoms, birds and bowers. . . .'"

Eddy groaned. "Oh, Mom, not now!" But it was too late. Once started, she could reel off poetry by the yard.

Undeterred, she went on: "''Of bridegrooms, brides and bridal cakes.' Robert Herrick, in case you wondered."

"Who asked?" Eddy said rudely.

"'Bridal cakes . . .'" Kate lifted her head and sniffed. "It smells gorgeous. Can't we stop here, Dad? The rain's over."

Desperate to distance himself from the cloaked man, Eddy burst out: "It's too close to Oxford!"

Kate stared. "What does that matter?"

"Well . . . I mean . . . look! There's no place to stop. We'd never get through the hedge."

Even as he spoke, he saw with dismay that a few feet further on the hedgerow ended in a stile. In spite of his protests they were soon settled in the grass, surrounded by a mountain of provisions.

Mrs. Newby began making sandwiches. Kate refused all nourishment with a martyred look and retired to some distance away. "So I won't be tempted." Out of the corner of his eye, Eddy saw her sneak a chocolate bar from her purse.

A watery sun broke through the clouds. Mingled scents of flowers, hay and clover drugged the air. Bees droned drowsily.

Eddy sat rigid, alert for anything. His imagination peopled the far side of each hedge and bush and tree with the cloaked figure. When a curious calf blew down his neck, he almost jumped out of his skin. Kate laughed, and he glared at her.

Desperately he filled his mouth and chewed. Sandwich after sandwich. His jaws ached with chewing.

"Slow down, Eddy," his mother cautioned. "You'll be sick if you eat so much."

He didn't answer. His brain worked with dismaying clarity. The cloaked man was following him! That much was clear. His turning up at the Wax Museum and Oxford couldn't have been coincidence. He had come, or been sent, after the statue. But how had he known where they were going? Was there a homing device in the statue? Why, oh, why hadn't Eddy just left it in the hotel? Why had he taken it in the first place? Would they never leave?

But if all the cloaked man wanted was the statue, why hadn't he taken it from him that first day? Did he want something else too? It was a chilling thought.

"I've got to go to the bathroom," Kate said.

"You've got the whole field," said Dr. Newby. He was stretched out full-length in the grass.

"Are you kidding?"

"Go behind a bush."

"What if a plane flies over?"

Reluctantly he stood up, brushing crumbs off his clothes.

Eddy started off with such alacrity, he cannoned into his mother who had bent to pluck something from the grass.

Smiling, she held out her hand. "Here, dear. A four-leaf clover. For good luck."

Did she really believe stuff like that? Nevertheless he took the tiny plant and tucked it in his pocket.

By midafternoon they were in Warwick. When they had registered at the hotel, Mrs. Newby said, "Hurry and unpack. We've got time to visit the castle before dinner."

Despite his worry, Eddy brightened. A castle. That was more like it. The word summoned visions of secret passages, torture chambers and dungeons with skeletons still drooping from their chains.

It was the work of minutes to dump his clothes into a drawer. "Done!" he announced, spilling paperbacks in an untidy heap on the bedside table.

Kate curled her lip. "What a mess! This place is a pigsty with all your junk. I wish we didn't have to share a room." She ignored his impatience as she folded and hung away her own extensive wardrobe with maddening care.

His disillusionment was swift and total. Whatever its warlike past, Warwick Castle now boasted acres of flow-

ered carpets, spindly gilt furniture, and crystal chande-
liers. No hapless corpses dangled from the walls; instead,
portraits of beruffled cavaliers sneered down at passing
tourists.

The sole excitement of the tour came when the guide
announced: "Now, ladies and gentlemen, in this very
room, in the year 1628, Lord Fulke Greville was murdered. And since those who die by violence are con-
demned to walk eternally, from that day to this his ghost
haunts these halls in search of vengeance. I, for one,
should not like to be here after dark!"

As they got ready for bed that night, Eddy grumbled.
"Some castle. More like a museum."

Kate turned from the mirror. She was always preening
herself these days, he noticed. He thought with a pang of
the time when she hadn't seemed to care how she looked.
They had been friends then. Real friends. Roughhousing.
Playing together. Sharing secrets. When had it changed?

He knew the answer all too well. When she'd gotten
boobs. And pimples. When all the dumb jocks from the
high school had started to hang around her. Talk about
wasting time!

To his astonishment, she agreed. "It wasn't much. I
thought there'd be dungeons. Oh, well. At least there was
a ghost."

"What ghost? Did you see him? They must think we're
jerks to fall for a line like that. Oh, what's the use? I didn't
ask to come. Why didn't they let me go camping?"

"Don't start that again!"

"Well, give me one good reason. Just one. I'm not a kid.
I oughta have some say."

"I can't figure out why you wanted to go camping. I

mean, rocks under your sleeping bag and ants in the food. Ugh! And Pete's okay. But his parents! His mom doesn't think about anything except playing tennis. And Mr. Anderson can't keep his hands to himself."

"What do you mean?"

She shuddered. "I stood next to him at the Smith's Christmas party. He was all over me! Patting and pinching and . . . if you don't believe me, ask Dad and Mom. They don't like you spending so much time there."

"It's none of their business. Yours, either. Besides, it's Pete that's my friend. Not his parents. And Dad and Mom aren't all that great. I mean, Dad tells those weird jokes and Mom spouts poetry and—"

"What're you complaining about? At least Dad takes you to the lab with him sometimes. Mom never comes to my basketball games. I guess she's ashamed of having a daughter who's a jock. That's for boys, not girls."

It stung. He laughed without amusement. "Yeah, well . . . But—you know what? Most times he just leaves me outside in the car. He says he has to check a gauge and he'll be back in a minute. Some minute!"

"Then why do you go?"

"Because he says he wants company. Because—" He stopped.

"Because what?"

"Nothing." How could he tell her he went hoping that somehow, someday his father would ask his help in those experiments that seemed to mean more to him than anything in the world? More than his own family.

"What do you do while you wait?"

"Read." He shrugged. "Then he complains I've always got my nose in a book."

She giggled.

"What's so funny?"

"You. I know what's really eating you. You think they turned down the camping trip because of your asthma. Well, for your information, Mom *was* worried about it. But Dad said to let you go. It was Pete's folks that said no."

"You're crazy. They invited me."

"No. Pete did. Without asking them first. They were scared you'd get sick somewhere out in the woods. With no doctor or hospital nearby. I don't blame them. Your attacks are scary."

He glared. How dared she talk like this? As if she knew things about him. Things he himself didn't know. It was *his* life! Not hers.

He stalked to his bed and got in, pulling the covers up over his head. But that didn't stop her. She went right on quacking at him. "You make me so furious! Everybody always takes care of you. You know what? I bet you make up those attacks, just to get attention."

Her voice died away at last. What seemed like aeons later, he poked his head up and looked around.

Night had not yet fully fallen. Outside, the last glow of summer twilight lingered. But under the eaves, the corners of the room were inky pools of darkness. The floorboards creaked and groaned as if to secret footsteps.

He lay back nervously and arranged himself for sleep. The bedclothes twisted and clung like jungle creepers. He tossed and turned, battling as if against human foes. Again he saw the pillow coming down. His breath caught.

In desperation he flopped over onto his stomach,

thrusting his toes deep into the cool crevasse between mattress and sheets.

After all, he consoled himself, *it wasn't Pete's fault. He wanted me even if his parents didn't. And she's wrong. I don't make up the asthma. But I wonder if other people think so too?*

In the street outside, a motorcycle roared. He swore, rolled over and sat up.

"Kate?"

The blanketed mound in the other bed did not stir.

"Kate!"

A sleepy voice snarled: "Whaddya want?"

It wasn't encouraging. But he could not bear to lie there, hating her. It was too lonely. He said tentatively, "I've got something to show you."

She only muttered unintelligibly.

"I found it at the market. It's a secret. No one knows about it yet." He waited, hugging himself with excitement. She had never been known to resist a secret.

Her response was a snore. The impulse to communicate died as quickly as it had been born. Probably it was better that way. No one would suspect the theft. And no one would make him return his treasure.

Suddenly his eyes widened. Why hadn't he seen it before? He had agonized over how to return the statue undetected. The truth was, he didn't mean to give it back! Not ever. It was his. It was meant to be his. No matter how he'd come by it. He would never return it. Cloaked man or no cloaked man.

Guilty but relieved, he lay back and closed his eyes. But sleep still eluded him. At last he stumbled out of bed and went to the closet. Kneeling in the dark, he unlocked the

44

suitcase and got out the statue. Clasping it defiantly, he returned to bed and fell instantly asleep.

Later—much later—he dreamed. He was alone. Groping down an endless, lightless corridor in Warwick Castle. By day it had been overcivilized. In dream it was transformed into a place of terror and decay. The fetid air was still. Too still. The uneasy calm before a storm. Under his stumbling feet live things scampered, squeaking and scuffling. He shivered with disgust. Something blundered past his face on frantic wings. He whirled, flailing, to fend it off.

His outstretched hands met stone. He jerked them back, fingers slimed and sticky. With an effort he forced them to explore further, until they traced the outlines of a doorway. His brain began to function again. Retreat along that corridor was unthinkable. The door was his only possible escape route.

He found the handle and tugged. Hinges squealed, but the door swung open and the blackness lightened somewhat. Through a window high on the far wall, moonlight cast its soft radiance, shining like a ship's lantern in fog.

As his eyes grew accustomed to the light, he took stock of his refuge. Recognition dawned, and with it horror. He was standing in the murder room!

The floorboards creaked behind him and he retreated deep into the room. Then he turned, heart in his mouth, to confront the danger.

The cloaked man was standing in the doorway! Eddy froze. Something—some tiny movement—betrayed him. The man started forward, head cocked and weaving, like a cobra about to strike. Only a few short paces separated his hands from Eddy's throat.

The light fell full on the man's face; Eddy recoiled. The man spoke: "You cannot escape me, Edward. I have killed you twice already!" The voice was the voice of the cloaked man. But the face was his father's.

Eddy tried to scream but no sound came. Without warning the floor gave way under him, and he and his pursuer were falling . . . falling . . . . Tumbling end over end into a vast dark silence.

He woke to find himself clutching the bed in a death grip as he choked and gasped.

"Eddy!" Kate was shaking him. "Wake up. It's okay now! I'm here. Please wake up." Her fingers gripped him frantically. "Here . . . wait a minute."

A switch clicked and the room was flooded with light. He blinked. Then she was beside him again, propping him with pillows.

"You'll breathe easier this way."

"My pills . . . the spray . . . in the bathroom."

She steadied his hands. When his breathing eased, she said, "I'll get Dad and Mom."

"No!"

"But Eddy . . ."

He caught at her arm. He couldn't face his father. Not yet. Not after the dream! He would never forget that face, that killer's face.

"Please, don't! I'm okay now. Honest. It was just a nightmare."

"Some nightmare." Her voice shook.

"I was at the castle. In the murder room. There was a man. . . ." He clutched at her. "He was going to strangle me. Like the princes." He frowned. "Only they were suffocated, weren't they? Under a pillow. But he said . . ."

46

"What did he say?"

"Nothing."

"It was just a dream. A nightmare."

Ashamed of his weakness, he pulled away. "I'm gonna get some sleep."

She still hovered. "Sure you don't need anything?"

All he wanted was to be left alone. But he didn't want to hurt her. "Thanks, Kate. I'm glad you were here."

She hugged him hard. "So'm I. 'Night, Eddy. Sleep tight and—"

"I know. Don't let the bedbugs bite."

He was more tired than he had ever been. Yet when she turned off the light he was still wakeful, content to listen to the curtains whisper in the night breeze.

His fingers moved restlessly, pleating and unpleating the bedclothes. Presently they encountered something solid. He hugged the statue to him, a more potent charm than any four-leaf clover. Now at last he slept, undreaming.

IV

He was fathoms deep, rocking on the blue-green currents of the ocean floor. The first light scarcely penetrated the sluggish shoals of sleep, nor did he heed the clamor of the birds outside the window.

Later, sunlight crawled across his pillow in a wide hot band, advancing with the passing minutes until the whole bed was lapped in warmth.

He screwed his eyes tight against the glare and burrowed deeper under the covers. But his nest had become uncomfortably hot. With an exclamation of protest he threw back the covers and stood up.

The room was quiet; Kate still slept. Grabbing up his clothes he staggered into the bathroom. The first shock of icy water cleared the mists from his brain. He forced himself to stand, letting the water sluice over him until his skin graveled with cold.

Shivering, he climbed out, toweled himself and dressed. But in the bedroom door he stopped, aghast. Kate was sitting on his bed, so engrossed in examination of the statue that she never looked up, even when he flew at her.

"Where'd you get that?" But he knew. He'd fallen asleep holding it. It must have been lying there in plain sight.

He made a wild grab. She stood up, holding the prize just out of reach.

"The question is, where'd you get it?" she demanded.

"Give it to me!"

"Not till you tell me."

"Okay, okay. At the street market. Now give it back." Again he lunged and missed.

"Did that Mrs.—what's her name—get it for you?"

"I bought it myself."

"Must have cost a fortune. Where'd you get the money?"

He blustered. "Saved it! I don't spend all my allowance on junk like you do. Anyway, the guy let me have it cheap. 'Cause it's broken. See?" It was half-true. And it sounded plausible.

To his surprise she didn't pursue it, saying only, "I wish you'd taken me with you."

"I thought you loved museums."

"Oh, that." Her tone conveyed disinterest.

He stared at her. "But I thought . . ."

It was her turn to lose her temper. "That's just it! You didn't think. You never do. You're so busy feeling sorry for yourself, you don't notice how anyone else feels." She checked herself. "Oh, Eddy, I'm sorry. 'Specially after last night. I know how tough it is, being sick so much. And Mom fussing and . . . But you're not the only one with problems. I can't go out on a date without their waiting up and asking if I had a good time. Oh, Mom tries to sound cool, but I know she's wondering if I got stoned or raped or something. Dad's worse. He doesn't say much, but if I'm a minute late, his lips get all tight and . . . well, you know what he's like! Once when I was wearing mascara he told me I looked like a tart." She looked at him. "Know what that is?"

"Of course," he said indignantly.

She went on as if she hadn't heard. "I dunno. Maybe it's because they're so old. I mean . . . getting married late and having us when they were past forty and . . ." She set the statue on the bureau with a thump and picked up her hairbrush. Heedless of snags she dragged it through her auburn mop until it crackled.

He retrieved his treasure and locked it away before she could change her mind. As he did so, that odd tingling ran up his arm again. He wondered if she had felt it. If so, she hadn't said. Then, reluctant to let the moment of sympathy die, he ventured, "Kate . . ."

"Umm . . ."

"Do you really want to know?"

"About what?"

"The statue, of course."

"I don't care."

He hesitated. But secrets were no fun unless you shared them. "Well, there was this guy wearing a long, dark cloak and . . ."

It was uphill work. He was wary, skirting the theft. She seemed almost indifferent now—fidgeting, pulling one dress after another from the closet only to discard it again.

His voice sank to a whisper. "He knew my name."

"What do you mean?"

"He knew it. Without my telling him."

"I don't believe you."

"It's true. He said it."

"He probably called you 'laddie.' That's British for 'sonny' or 'boy.'"

"He said 'Edward.' 'Farewell, Edward.' Another thing. He'd seen the statue before."

"How do you know?"

"The way he looked at it. Something he said."

"So what? You met him at the market. He's probably another antiques dealer. Like the woman. I'll bet he'd had his eye on the statue himself. And you took it right out from under his nose. No wonder he followed you."

"What about the name?"

"Maybe he heard you and the woman talking."

"But I . . ." He thought of the staring eyes, the stealthy footsteps he had dismissed as imaginary. He gulped. "Kate . . ."

"What now?"

"He's still following me!"

She raised her eyebrow. "Oh?"

It goaded him. "Remember the guy I saw at Tussaud's—in the scene with the princes? That was him. And in Oxford yesterday, he walked out of a house and right up to the car and . . ." He faltered. "At least I think it was him."

"How come I never saw him?"

"You were in the market."

"And at Tussaud's?"

He shook his head despairingly. "I didn't see him myself until you'd gone."

"You'd think one of us would have. Dressed like that. If there's any such person."

"There is! And he's following me. Honest, Kate!"

"Why would he keep following you?"

It was the one question he couldn't answer. Not without confessing his crime.

She turned back to the mirror. "Wouldn't you know? A pimple coming out on my chin."

He tried again. "I'm not making it up. I did see him."

"You've gotta admit it's hard to believe. Some guy dresses up like a spook and no one but you sees him and—"

"Drop dead!" He slammed out of the room.

At breakfast he picked at his food, pushing eggs and sausage round and round until the plate was crisscrossed with slimy tracks.

"For heaven's sake," his mother snapped finally, "eat it or leave it, but stop playing with it!" A worried frown creased her forehead. "You're so pale! You're not getting sick, are you?"

"I didn't sleep well. That's all." He glared at Kate, daring her to betray him. But she held her peace.

Dr. Newby poured the coffee. "We have a full day planned. Tonight we're going to Stratford to see a play. And this morning I thought we'd run over to Coventry to see the cathedral. It was bombed in the war, but they've made a shrine out of the ruin."

Another church, Eddy thought. He avoided his father's eye. Somehow he could not look at him without remembering the moonlit face of his dream. The talons reaching hungrily for his throat.

Later, standing in the ruined cathedral, he still could not control a shrinking when his father spoke beside him. He stole a quick glance, hoping against hope his father's face would be back to normal. But it was rigid, angry. Words pushed through the tight lips like weapons. "This was terrorism, pure and simple! It wasn't a military target." Before his fury Eddy recoiled, as if it had been meant for him.

He sought his mother's eye. To his dismay her face too

was different, distorted with sadness and an uncharacteristic rage.

Once more he was overwhelmed by the need to escape. He had to get away. He looked around. The old tower still stood, monument to a night of fire and destruction, guarding the shattered open space that once had been the church.

"I'm gonna climb up. Take a look around."

"Do you really think . . . You get so out of breath." His mother's worry was palpable. He shook off her restraining hand. Was he never to be free?

As he began to climb, his father's nightmare mask receded. The surge of muscles responding to his will soothed him.

Round and round and round. Each spiral of stone steps followed hard upon the last. Upward. Ever upward. Soon his knees were trembling, his breath came raggedly. He kept his eyes riveted to the next step, lest the distance still ahead defeat his purpose.

Quite suddenly the climb was at an end. He opened a door and found himself outside on the balcony that encircled the base of the spire. Tipping his head back he squinted up at the weather vane. Against the racing clouds, the spire seemed to tilt and topple.

About him cathedral daws and rooks circled, spiraling and looping on the air currents. He watched enviously. How easy it looked. He could almost believe himself weightless, released from gravity's heavy bonds. He had only to spread his wings, to hurl himself outward. . . . Then he too would swoop and soar, insubstantial as a feather on the wind.

The air was cool against his hot cheeks. Air, a magic

carpet. His friend, for once. Never again to battle for it, groveling and gasping. To be its master, not its slave. Air, the ultimate prize!

His hands tightened on the parapet. His muscles tensed, ready to propel him up and over. For once the voice in his head was silent.

Reality broke over him like an icy wave! He wrenched himself back, trembling. Long moments passed before he brought himself to look down. At the real world. At safety.

When at last he did, he saw figures scuttling across the pavement like so many agitated beetles. He could make out his father bending over a piece of sculpture. Kate and his mother rested on a bench nearby. Kate's hair flamed copper in the sunlight. Mrs. Newby looked up and waved. Weak with relief, Eddy waved back.

As he watched, a man appeared. He strode to the altar and dropped to his knees in prayer. The stuff of his cloak poured out in sculptured folds behind him.

For an instant Eddy was transfixed. Then he turned and hurled himself at the steps. His footsteps echoed like thunder in the enclosed stairwell. He forced past a party of ascending tourists, ignoring their indignant mutters: "Snotty kid! Who does he think he is?"

Halfway down, he stumbled and fended himself off the wall with his fists. Heedless of torn knuckles, he hurried on. This time he would not run away. This time he would confront the cloaked man. Demand that he leave him alone!

Kate met him as he emerged at the base of the tower. "You sure got down fast! Ever thought of trying out for track?

He brushed past her. "Where is he?"

Her smile faded. "Who?"

"The cloaked man."

"Oh, Eddy! Don't start that again."

He grabbed her arm. "You must have seen him. He walked right past you."

She shook her head.

He turned to his father. "You saw him, didn't you? He was in front of the altar. Praying." His voice rose.

"Simmer down, son. Who are you talking about?"

"The man." He appealed to his mother. "Wearing a long dark cloak. Like the academic robes you told us about."

"I'm sorry, dear. I suppose the sun got in your eyes." She put a hand on his arm. "The exercise seems to have done you good."

Desperately he shook her off. There was disbelief, suspicion on all their faces. Kate looked at once wary and smug. As always when she had the inside track. He cursed the weakness that had led him to confide in her.

"It's almost lunchtime," Dr. Newby said. "We'd better go."

On the drive back to Warwick Eddy was silent, lost in thought. By the time they reached the hotel, his mind was made up. He would say nothing more. No matter what. They wouldn't believe him anyway, so what was the point?

Through lunch he did his best to steer the talk to safe channels. But when he got up, Kate was at his side. She took his arm, saying smoothly, "Don't worry about us this afternoon. We'll take care of ourselves. I'll see he gets cleaned up for the theater."

He had no chance to escape. She stuck like a leech, hustling him upstairs and locking the room door after them, then pocketing the key.

"Now," she said. "Is this your idea of a joke?"

"I told you. The guy was in Coventry today."

She shook her head. "Uh-uh! You can't get away with it this time. We were all there. None of us saw him."

Despite his resolve, he was stung to protest. "But you must have!"

She smiled knowingly.

Hanging on to his temper, he said, more to himself than to her, "I don't get it. I just don't get it."

Her face softened. "Listen, Eddy, maybe you should tell Dad."

"I tried to this morning. He didn't believe me."

"No, I mean the whole story. About how you met the man . . . and the statue and everything. Because if he's some kind of crook, or a crazy . . . Well, Dad could go to the police."

He turned cold. The police would go to the market. To the shop. And the shopkeeper knew the statute was stolen. Probably he had sent the cloaked man after him.

At all costs, he had to head her off. Before she started the ball rolling to disaster.

He forced a laugh. "It's not as bad as all that. And I'd feel like a jerk if I were wrong."

She didn't seem to be listening. "He might even turn out to be a homicidal maniac. An ax murderer! Like in the movies." Her face shone with excitement.

Trying to sound nonchalant, he said, "I guess I'll have to chance it."

She hadn't believed him earlier. Now she had the bit

between her teeth. "Come to think of it, maybe I did see—"

"Drop it!" he snapped. "Just forget I said anything." Then, in desperation, because she couldn't seem to let go: "You were right! It was a joke. A bad joke. And you fell for it!"

He flopped down on the bed in a show of unconcern. His hand fell on his Tolkien. It opened automatically to a well-worn page. He pretended absorption, peeking out from time to time from under his lashes.

Kate was staring at him, face registering bewilderment and exasperation. He kept his eyes glued to the book but he was sharply conscious of her gaze. It seemed an eternity before she turned away.

He went on, flipping pages unseeingly, but after a time the old familiar magic gripped him, and he rode with Frodo, fleeing the Black Riders of Mordor. "Go back," Frodo cried. "Go back to Mordor and follow me no more!"

"Follow me no more." The words had taken on a new and personal significance. He knew now how it felt to be hunted. In the book it was heroic. In real life it was terrifying. He felt very small and lonely.

He had counted on his family to right his troubles. Now he bore a burden he could not share. And some lingering childishness within cried: *Never? Not ever again?* While that voice snarled: *You crazy? D'ya wanna go to jail?*

But Frodo had had his quest. And even at the blackest moments, Samwise had been at his side. Eddy's hard-won freedom seemed to him a poor exchange for such companionship. Rare tears stung his eyes.

He must have dozed off because Kate shook him awake to get ready for the theater. As they hurried through the lobby, he asked, "What play are we seeing?"

"*Richard the Third*," his mother said. "You'll like it. It's good old-fashioned melodrama."

The house lights were already dimming as they took their seats. The air was sibilant with whispers and the rustle of programs. At the last minute another latecomer seated himself nearby. The theater was warm, but the man made no move to take off the cloak he clutched so tightly to him.

Urgently Eddy turned to Kate; even as he opened his mouth, trumpets blared, the house lights were extinguished and the curtain rose on the play.

A slight figure dressed in black limped down to the footlights. With his first words the suspense in the theater became electric. Was it voice—by turns harsh and wooing—or words that cast the spell? Eddy did not know. He knew only that each nerve, each atom of consciousness was riveted on the figure. Although at some deeper level, he remained uneasily aware of the cloaked man so close-by.

As the play unfolded, Richard plotted, ensnaring all who crossed his path—wife, brothers, nephews, friends—in the web of his ambition. Like some venomous spider, he darted, scuttled, pounced upon his prey.

In the audience, tension mounted. Eddy squirmed, feeling the disapproval, even hatred, growing in the air about him. For some reason it made him uncomfortable. What did they know? What did any of them know of how it felt to be small and sick and scorned? Unexpected laughter shook him.

"Shh!" Kate hissed. "What's the matter with you? It's not funny."

What was wrong with him? She was right. Plots, betrayals, murders—they weren't funny at all. Yet with each new outrage, each crime, his heart leapt treacherously. His throat was thick with cheers. Hoarse animal shouts, the kind Pete and he laughed at at football games. Dumb jocks!

At intermission he followed the others out into the lobby. Blinking in the light, he dared a furtive look about. But the cloaked man was nowhere to be seen.

"Juice?" His mother offered a small carton. He gulped it down thirstily.

"Wonderful performance," his father said.

His wife nodded. "Richard is magnificent. Evil personified."

"He's revolting," Kate said flatly. "Like a tarantula. Ugh!"

Eddy was moved to protest. "He couldn't help it."

"What do you mean?" All their eyes were on him.

He was hot with shame. How could he explain? That all Richard needed was to be let to breathe. Not to be looked down on for his size and sickliness.

He shifted ground. "At least he knew what he wanted. And how to get it."

"The end justifies the means. Is that it?" his father said. "Every tyrant in history has used that tired excuse." His face looked as it had that morning. Disapproving. Angry.

"Now, John," said Mrs. Newby. "I'm sure that's not what Eddy meant. It's just that Richard is so powerful, he sweeps you along with him."

Was that it? Was that really all?

"Why," she went on, "it's proof of Shakespeare's genius that he makes a monster so compelling. Just wait, though, Eddy. You'll see it differently when the princes are killed. It's heartbreaking."

"When's that?" He tried not to sound eager.

"They're killed offstage. One of their killers describes it. Even so, it's all too graphic."

"Oh, well," he said, "I expect the brats deserved it." Half-gleeful, half-apprehensive, he waited for the storm to break.

It was not long in coming. The outrage on all their faces told him this time he had gone too far. He did not dare look at his father, but his mother was visibly shocked.

"Talk about brats!" Kate spluttered. "Takes one to know one! You've just about ruined the trip."

"Kate!" Mrs. Newby reproved.

Her eyes filled. "I'm sorry, Mom. But he's impossible. You should try sharing a room with him. Anyway it's all your fault. Yours and Dad's. You both let him get away with murder. Just because he has asthma." Her voice broke. As the tears spilled over she hurried back into the theater.

The silence that fell lasted until the buzzer for the next act. As they took their places, Eddy sneaked a look for the cloaked man. But his seat was still empty.

I don't care, he told himself stubbornly. *I meant it. Richard wasn't so bad. They just hated him because he was braver and stronger than they were. Even though he was little and crippled.*

Now scene followed scene with the momentum of a roller coaster. At last the fatal moment came, and Richard's henchman slouched downstage to tell of the killings. His words spoke of a "tyrannous and bloody act." His manner told a different tale. Relaxed and businesslike, it invited his listeners to share in the pride of a task well done.

Eddy's stomach tensed. Whether from excitement or horror, he was not sure. Once more the boys rose up before him in their helpless terror. Once more he writhed and struggled under that suffocating pillow!

Someone was watching. He tore his eyes from the stage to look directly into the cloaked man's stare. He half rose.

"Sit down!" Kate ordered. "It's not over yet."

As she spoke, the cloaked man got to his feet and strode from the theater.

The play drove on to its inevitable climax. In the last act, Richard made ready to defend his stolen crown. Now he was tormented by an agony of doubt. One by one his enemies rose up on the eve of battle, confronting him with prophecies of defeat and death.

On Bosworth field, two armies clashed in mortal combat. The king's courage reasserted itself. Facing sure disaster, he hurled one last defiance at the world: "I have set my life upon a cast, And I will stand the hazard of the die."

His words flared through Eddy's blood like wildfire. Drunk with excitement, he dared to hope that somehow, someway, the king would still win through. Yet in the end he fell, fighting alone amongst his enemies.

Driving back through the summer night Eddy rehearsed those last scenes over and over. Courage. A steely will. Contempt for the opinions of others. Richard had had all of these in good measure. Could Eddy ever hope to match him?

V

They overslept the next day and it was late before they got under way. Though Eddy swore he had barely fallen asleep before his mother was shaking him awake again. He fumbled into his clothes, packed and absorbed rather than ate breakfast—all in a state of semi-consciousness.

Dr. Newby apologized as they pulled away. "I know you'd rather have slept in. But we must make Nottingham tonight for me to get to the conference tomorrow. On the way we'll stop at Bosworth to see the battlefield."

Kate stifled a yawn. " 's it still there?"

"Of course, stupid," Eddy told her. "Places don't disappear."

His mother turned to frown. "Watch your language. We've had enough bickering. And, yes, Kate—according to the guidebook the battlefield is on a farm."

"Umm." Kate's head nodded. She uttered a gentle snore.

Eddy eyed her with disfavor. Trust a girl to fall asleep on the way to a battlefield. "D'you think we'll find anything? Like swords or arrowheads or . . ."

His father shook his head. "It's been over five hundred years. It's probably long since picked over. Not to speak of the seasonal ploughing and planting. Still, we can spy out the lay of the land. Some of those battle scenes were a little unclear."

62

"For a man who claims to hate war," his wife said tartly, "you certainly are fascinated by all the gory details."

In the rearview mirror, Eddy caught his father's eye. They exchanged a rueful grin. The complaint was familiar as a well-worn sneaker.

"It's strategy, Mom," he explained. "Like in chess. Or football."

They drove on in silence. Mrs. Newby looked at her watch. "Shouldn't we be there by now?"

"I'm not sure," Dr. Newby confessed.

She seemed more pleased than upset. "Then we're lost!"

Kate woke with a start. "I'm hungry."

"All right, all right," Dr. Newby grumbled, "I get the message. I'll make inquiries first chance I get."

They found a post office in a nearby town. Dr. Newby disappeared inside to return in minutes, looking smug.

"Just as I thought. This is Market Bosworth. The battlefield is two miles south, on a farm between Shenton and Sutton Cheney. They suggest we also stop to see the church where Richard and his officers heard mass on their way to battle."

"Would you believe that?" Kate whispered. "He didn't have the foggiest idea. But here we are!"

Eddy threw her a frosty stare. He hadn't yet forgiven her words the night before.

She looked abashed. "I'm sorry, Eddy. I always seem to lose my temper with you, but . . ."

His attention had already wandered. Since his father had announced their destination, he'd been distracted.

Living and reliving the play's last moments. For the first time since that day in London, the cloaked man and the statue had receded from his mind.

Kate was still gabbling. Now she wound up: ". . . the nerve to defend him." She looked at him expectantly.

What on earth was she talking about? He racked his brains. He had it! He said, "You know how people make a big deal about athletes who stage a comeback after getting hurt?"

"What's that got to do with it?"

"Don't you see? Richard was crippled. But that didn't stop him. He became a great soldier anyway."

"If you're defending him because he was a cripple," his mother put in, "forget it. It wasn't so."

"What do you mean? You saw him. He was all twisted up and lame and . . ."

"In the play. It makes for good melodrama. And it's probably what Shakespeare believed. After all, he never saw him. He lived a hundred years later. But contemporary accounts show that at most one of his shoulders was higher than the other. His sword arm. Which would be natural, since he'd been a soldier since he was thirteen."

"That's just a kid!" Kate exclaimed.

"It wasn't unusual in those days. Children grew up fast. They had to. Life was short. And Richard's family always had to fight for survival. He'd been his brother Edward's commander-in-chief since he was a boy. I suppose there was no one else to trust."

If only I had lived then! thought Eddy.

John Newby said, "Since when have you become an expert?"

"I picked up a biography of Richard when I bought the

64

tickets. After we got back last night, I read it straight through. Fascinating! Did you know some people don't think he killed the princes? There's no proof. They never found the bodies."

He laughed. "Well, as the Warder said, they never came out alive. How much more proof do you need?"

"The author argues it wasn't in character. Even his worst enemies admitted he was loyal to his brother. And these were his brother's children."

"He could have adored the brother and been jealous of the kids."

"Why should Shakespeare lie?" Kate asked.

"Maybe he didn't know it was a lie. He simply retold the story he had heard."

Kate's eyes danced with excitement. She looked at Eddy. "This is turning out to be a real mystery! Maybe you were right all along. Maybe . . ."

"But I didn't say . . ."

"Don't jump to conclusions," his father warned. "There's no proof Richard didn't kill them either. The plain fact is, they disappeared and Richard became king. That's the sort of simple evidence scientists like. The rest is speculation. Fairy tales."

"Oh, bother scientists!" snapped his wife.

Dr. Newby reddened. Eddy wished she wouldn't bait him. His rage could be fearsome. But he smiled finally, and slowed the car to lean out and read the road sign.

"Sutton Cheney and Shenton. Can't be much further."

Eddy was silent. He felt oddly deflated. Richard's villainy had been exhilarating. Now, if his mother were right, he was diminished. Just a small man who had fought and ruled and died defeated.

"Small." The word reverberated. Small and crippled. Or maybe not crippled. But unloved. Hated even. Appealing in his bitterness. At that moment more real to Eddy than his own family. Almost a friend. They would have understood each other.

"I think we should skip the church and push on to the battlefield," his mother said suddenly. "It looks as if a storm is coming up."

The sky had darkened. Under banks of heavy pewter cloud, the wind lashed the trees along the roadside into a frenzy.

They swung off the main road and climbed a steep lane. At the crest they parked beside a fence and got out.

"Now what?" Kate said, vainly trying to contain her flying hair.

Dr. Newby pointed. "Over that gate and through the farmyard."

"That's trespassing," Mrs. Newby protested.

"They said at the post office that everyone does it."

"Come on!" Eddy urged, in a fever of impatience.

The yard was muddy. Kate and Mrs. Newby picked their way between cow pies with expressions of disgust. Eddy thought they looked like minesweepers crossing a perilous field.

A little further on, the way was barred by barbed wire.

"That does it!" said Kate. "I'm not going over, under, or through that stuff. I tore my last pair of pantyhose on that dumb gate. Let's go back to the car."

Eddy found a loose strand of wire. "Come on," he coaxed. "I'll hold it for you." Even as he spoke, something cold and wet plopped onto his nose.

Kate whirled and ran. She covered the return in record

time, this time managing the stile without mishap. Though she could be heard lamenting: "My hair! It'll frizz."

"Coming, Eddy?" Dr. Newby asked.

"Nope."

"All right. But don't be long. We'll wait in the car."

He turned his back on them and slogged on. Soon he came to a stone cairn. Blinking the rain from his eyes, he read the commemorative plaque:

NEAR THIS SPOT, ON AUGUST 22, 1485, AT THE AGE OF THIRTY-TWO, RICHARD THE THIRD FELL FIGHTING GALLANTLY IN DEFENSE OF HIS REALM AGAINST THE USURPER HENRY TUDOR.

As he walked on, the rain drove full in his face. A tangle of roses grew wild here; their fragile petals whirled like snowflakes on the gusting wind. The thorns caught at him; he wrenched himself free.

Excitement had turned to melancholy. Richard had died a young man. Younger than Eddy's father. Had he ridden out expecting victory that summer morning? Or had he guessed he was to die? Had John Newby gone to war in hope or fear so many years before? What if he, like Richard, had never come home? A lump of ice formed in Eddy's stomach at the thought.

A clump of trees loomed at the crest of a small hill. Instinctively he swerved toward them. His passing flushed a covey of birds from the thicket; they darted up, wings beating the air in panic.

The ground was rough, the grass long and tussocky. Slipping and slithering in his wet sneakers, he struggled on. By the time he reached the hilltop, he was panting.

The branches cut the full force of wind and rain here, creating a leafy oasis in the storm's eye. He fished out a handkerchief and mopped his face.

"We meet again, lad!"

Eddy whirled, hands raised as if to ward off a blow.

The cloaked man stood a few feet from him. "Afraid, boy? Of me?" There was incredulity in his voice. More than that, sharp hurt. "I shall not harm you."

Eddy looked wildly around. Could he outrun him to the car? He knew he could not. He quavered: "What do you want?"

The man didn't answer for a moment. Then he said, "Only to talk with you." There was no menace there.

The impulse to flight died, leaving bewilderment and growing anger in its wake. Eddy said, "I'm not giving it back. No matter what you do."

His companion seemed taken aback. "Of course. Who has a better right to it than you?"

It was Eddy's turn to be surprised. His uneasiness began to rise again. If the man did not want the statue, what then?

"Listen," said the other abruptly. "Do you hear them?"

It had stolen on him almost unawares; now he realized that for some time he had been conscious of a rumbling. Like the sound of distant thunder. Or gunfire. Then with a thrill of excitement and fear he recognized it for what it was—horses' hooves, hundreds of them massed in charge. The sound came on and on. Beating on his ears, his brain, his heart!

"It's a stampede!" he shouted. "Coming this way. Let's get out of here."

The man did not move.

Eddy strained to see them through the rain and mist. But already the din was diminishing. At last it faded into a sullen muttering, to die away altogether. Now only the steady drip . . . drip . . . drip of raindrops on the leaves overhead broke the stillness.

"Come," said the cloaked man. "I will show you the battlefield."

"Where'd they go?"

"Come."

"But I heard them."

"Do not be afraid. They are gone. Now come with me."

Stubbornly he hung back. "I said I'd only be gone a little."

"Do you not wish to see the field?"

Eddy flushed. "Have you been here before?"

The man smiled. A tight cold smile that did not reach his eyes. "Many times." He pointed in the direction Eddy had come from. "You saw the well?"

"What well?"

"At the cairn."

He nodded.

"It is called Dickon's Well. The King drank there before riding into battle. And the trees under which we stand are called King Dick's Clump. It was here he raised his standard for the final charge. The last charge of the last Plantagenet King of England."

The words seemed to hang there. As real as the band of knights that waited—pressing close—to follow their royal master on the fatal ride. The horses, sensing battle, pawed and stamped nervously. The feral smells of sweat and fear were heavy on the air.

"Loyauté me lie," the man murmured.

"What's that?"

The tawny eyes considered him. "You do not remember? It was Richard's motto. The one he chose for himself. "Loyalty binds me." He was silent a minute, then added, "Fitting words for him and those who followed him to death that day. This place is Ambion Hill. Richard led them from this crest down through the battle lines and across the swampy ground that separated the two armies. Then up yonder slope"—he pointed—"and at the enemy!" He strode away downhill.

Eddy followed, almost running to keep up. The cloaked man did not spare a backward glance, but his words came clearly: "Straight as the arrow's deadly flight, straight at Henry Tudor's heart!" Again he raised an arm to point. "There Richard fell, surrounded by his foes. Betrayed. Murdered by a band of traitors!" His voice had risen. With the next words it dropped till Eddy could barely hear him. "Yonder is Crown Hill. The Tudor's lackeys crowned him there. Set upon his head the golden circlet Richard bore upon his battle helm."

"What happened then?"

"Then? Why then, for Richard the long agony was over. Does it matter what came next?"

They walked on for a time. Suddenly the man exclaimed and bent to pick something from the grass. He held it out.

"Take it, lad."

"What is it?"

"A sword point. Broken off in battle."

"Swords can't break." Even as Eddy spoke he thought

70

of the knight on horseback. But that was old and made of wood. "I mean, steel can't."

The man smiled. "The hardest steel may shatter. Cleaving armor. Or bone."

Reluctantly Eddy held his hand out. Without touching him the man dropped the shard into his palm. It was icy cold. Eddy stared at it in fascinated horror. So small a thing to kill a man. A living breathing human like himself. Ending in one second's agony the warmth of blood and breath and life. Lodging in the brain, perhaps. Flesh and bone had wasted, leaving only this behind. The edge was discolored. Was it rust? Or was it stained with blood?

He recoiled. "I don't want it."

The grim face softened. "I had forgotten. You were ever mindful of another's pain. Yet keep it, Edward. For my sake. Keep it and remember always."

It was then that Eddy heard them again. Horses' hooves. This time no more than the slow *clip-clop* . . . *clip-clop* . . . *clip-clop* of one lone horse. A tired animal stumbling along a stony track.

Instinctively Eddy drew aside to let it pass. Presently the sound faded into silence once more.

The cloaked man stared after the invisible beast. He said softly, "They bore Richard dead into Leicester. Flung naked and bleeding over a pack horse, a felon's halter round his neck. His herald rode before. Henry had commanded it. They say the herald wept. But Richard could no longer weep. Yet his wounds wept blood."

Eddy found he could not speak. He rubbed his eyes hard, hoping the other wouldn't notice. When he was sure of his voice, he said, "I don't understand. It was five hundred years ago. But I heard them. The war horses. And the one carrying Richard's body. Where'd they go?"

"Back where they belong!" was the savage response.

He winced. But the man had turned away to gaze into the distance. He seemed to have forgotten Eddy's presence.

"Eddy! Where are you?" It was his father's voice.

The alarm sounded in his head, urgent as a fire bell. His father and the cloaked man must not meet!

"I've got to go."

There was no reply.

He tried again. "We're going to Nottingham." He broke off, appalled at what he had revealed. He had blurted it out as if . . . as if he wanted the man to know.

The man smiled that thin-lipped smile. The frown lines on his forehead deepened. "Nottingham," he repeated, as if trying to remember. "Nottingham. Castle of My Care."

"I don't understand."

"No matter. We shall not meet in Nottingham, Edward."

"Edward Newby! Do you hear me? Get back here on the double!"

Still he hung back. Waiting. But the man seemed to have retreated to some dark dream of his own. He made no effort to keep him.

At last Eddy started back, struggling through the long grass. His jeans clung limply to his legs. With each step his sodden sneakers squelched.

On Ambion Hill he stopped to draw breath. The mists had thickened over the low ground, and when he looked back he could only just make out the cloaked man, still standing motionless where he had left him.

Striking out downhill, Eddy ran full tilt into John Newby bearing down on him.

"Where have you been?" he demanded. "I've shouted myself hoarse."

"I'm sorry, Dad. I was wandering around. I guess I lost track of the time."

"You picked quite a day for it! Look at you. You're soaked! Probably come down with a whopper of a cold." An unwilling smile tugged at his mouth. "Oh, well. No sense borrowing trouble. I'd have done the same thing at your age. Though I didn't have asthma."

Eddy flushed.

His father sighed. "Sorry. I know you don't like to be reminded. To tell the truth, if your mother and Kate hadn't been here, I'd have come with you. Find any souvenirs?"

He shook his head. He couldn't share the sword point. Any more than he could the statue. Or the cloaked man. "No!" It came out more harshly than he meant.

There was a pause. He tried desperately to think of something to repair the damage.

His father said finally, "All right, son. Let's get back. Your mother must be worried." His shoulders sagged as if he were tired.

Back in the car Eddy's cheeks burned from the wind, but his hands and feet were icy. He dug his fists into his pockets to warm them. One hand met the fragment of metal. Deliberately he drew his thumb across the edge, trying not to wince as the flesh caught and tore. What was it like to be wounded in battle? Surreptitiously he examined the gash, licking away the welling blood.

A little further on they drew up at an inn. "Time to

eat," Mrs. Newby said. "And you two can dry out."

The wind caught the front door, slamming it behind them. They huddled in the semidarkness of the hallway. A fat woman bustled toward them, drying her hands on her apron as she came.

"Dreadful weather, isn't it? More like November than July. But there, I mustn't keep you in this draughty hall. There's a good fire in the bar parlor. Come and warm yourselves. I'll see to something to eat."

She led them into a long whitewashed room. From the blackened ceiling beams hung batteries of pots and pans. The metal winked rosily in the firelight.

At one end of the room stood the bar; at the other, a huge fireplace was set into the chimney breast. The hearth was so large, it easily held benches on either side of the logs. Over the mantel hung a tarnished sword. With a sudden catch of breath, Eddy saw the point was broken off.

"Help me pull this chair up to the fire," the woman said. "There's a good lad. My joints are that bad today!" She touched his shoulder and exclaimed: "Had a proper wetting, haven't you! Looks like someone went to the well once too often." Chuckling at her own witticism, she deposited him in the chair's prickly plush lap. "There now. Sit and dry yourself. I'll fetch something hot." Moving with surprising speed for one of her bulk, she squeezed through the door to the right of the hearth and disappeared.

Mrs. Newby's face was alight with pleasure. "Just look at those beams. They must have been old when the Armada sailed."

"I don't know about that," said Kate, "but I'm going to

74

try one of the benches in the fireplace. I'm frozen. Coming, Eddy?"

He shook his head. Outside the rain beat monotonously against the windows. The logs crackled; flames leapt and fell. His eyelids drooped.

"Drink this," said the woman in his ear. "It'll put color in those pale cheeks."

He gulped. Fiery liquid ran down his throat. Tears spurted into his eyes; he choked and spluttered.

The woman grinned. "Real tea! Stewed all day on the back of the stove. Not like the slops they serve in tearooms."

He peered into the mug. The brew was dark, more like coffee than the golden beverage his mother served. He sipped more cautiously this time. It scorched his throat, but a core of warmth radiated through his chilled body.

Idly he glanced down at his feet and stiffened. His sneakers were daubed with stains. Rusty stains. He thought of the unseen horse that had passed so close he might have touched it. A horse bearing Richard's body, wounds still weeping blood!

Numb with shock, he heard his mother's voice from somewhere far away. "Have you had the inn for long?"

"Been in the family nigh on five hundred years. But my man's dead in Africa in the war, and we'd no children. So I'm the last."

Eddy managed to say, "Was your family here when"— he cleared his throat—"when the battle was fought?"

"Bosworth? That'll be where you got that wetting. It's no fit day for climbing fences and walking through the long grass. I see by your jacket you've been through the wire, too. Or the roses. Wicked, them thorns! Yes, young man, my people fought at Bosworth. Alongside of most folks from hereabouts. Elmerthorpe, Earl Shilton, Market Bosworth, Shenton, Sutton Cheney." Her face clouded. "A sad day for England that were."

"You mean they fought for Richard?"

"Who else?"

"What about the murdered princes?" Dr. Newby said in a shocked voice.

A mulish look crossed her face. "Don't know about that, sir. All I know is, he's known in these parts as Good King Dick. An Englishman trueborn. Which is more than can be said of that mean meaching Welsh jackanapes Henry Tudor!" Her scorn was withering. "Come right through the fields in August. Trampled down the ripe corn with his soldiers and their horses, instead of marching them up the lane like any decent Englishman would have done." She pointed to the sword. "See that? They do say it were found on the field. I've always hoped the point were right where it belongs to be. In one of them thick Welsh skulls! Now, if you'll come into the dining room, I've a nice bit of cheese, and eggs and fresh-baked scones for your tea."

Eddy lingered. As if drawn by a magnet he approached the mantel. Unwillingly, he reached into his pocket for the sword fragment. He was shaking with suspense when he held it up. It fit as neatly as the missing segment of a jigsaw puzzle!

He started as his mother spoke behind him. "Come, dear. We're waiting for you."

"Sorry. I . . . uh . . . wanted to see the sword up close." Hoping she hadn't noticed, he stuffed the bit of metal back into his pocket.

She said disapprovingly, "What a character! Like something out of an English novel. A bit bloodthirsty for my taste, but I suppose you lapped it up. Imagine feeling so strongly after five hundred years!"

He did not answer. As clearly as if he were in the room he heard the cloaked man speaking: *Keep it, Edward. For my sake. Keep it and remember always.*

VI

The morning traffic was heavy in Nottingham. As their cab idled, immobilized by the crush that clogged the streets, Eddy began to regret the impulse to accompany his father to the lab.

Dr. Newby had been dubious from the start. "I don't think you'll find it all that interesting. Nothing dramatic. Not like scientists on TV."

"I know. But I want to go anyway. At home I never get a chance to see what you do. Not really."

His mother had been frankly annoyed. "Kate and I are going to Nottingham Castle to see the Robin Hood statues. I thought you'd jump at the chance. Besides . . ."

He waited.

The real reason was not slow to surface. "I'm not sure you should be out and around today. I don't like the sound of that cough. Not one bit!"

Beside him, his father was silent, absorbed—as usual—in a sheaf of papers. Presently he took out his calculator. His fingers flew on the keys.

Eddy cleared his throat. There was no answer.

He said, so loudly he startled himself, "Who're we going to see?"

"What? Oh, just a sec . . . I want to finish this."

He had hoped it would be different. That today his father would take him in, initiate him into the mysteries of his beloved science. At home, whenever Eddy ventured into John Newby's study, he was greeted by the back of his head, haloed in the cold light of the fluorescent desk lamp. He would sidle over to stand beside him, racking his brains for a topic, anything to lure his attention. Sometimes he stood there for half an hour or more. Occasionally Dr. Newby would look up and smile. But always he turned back to his work. Until in the end Eddy gave up and tiptoed away.

He tried again. "Do you know someone at this lab?"

"Ronald Knowlton. A pharmaceutical chemist. We've been corresponding since he read my last article. His research interests me."

"What kind of research?"

"In broad-spectrum antibiotics. And allergies. Both present problems of . . ."

Eddy brightened. After all, it might be all right. For once his father seemed eager to talk. Yet as he talked, his words grew more and more incomprehensible. Until Eddy's eyes glazed, and he thought despairingly, Might as well be talking Chinese.

"So, you see," his father wound up, "since every element has its own atomic fingerprint . . ."

Fingerprint at least sounded promising. Like something out of Sherlock Holmes!

They drew up at a grimy factory complex. A pudgy man paced by the front gate. Without waiting for them to get out, he flung open the cab door and reached in to pump Dr. Newby's hand.

"Well, Newby! Well, well, well. Well met."

Eddy had begun to wonder if he knew another word when the man turned to him.

"Well. What have we here?"

"This is my son, Edward. He came along to see your lab."

"A budding scientist! Though"—Ronald Knowlton frowned—"safety rules, don't you know. Uh . . . no kiddies allowed. Still, I suppose we can find somewhere for him to wait." He brightened. "Of course! The candy machine. You like candy, don't you, son?" He poked Eddy. "Could use a bit of fattening, by the look of you." He hiked his trousers firmly over his own generous paunch.

Eddy said nothing. His father's lips tightened. In total silence they followed their chuckling host through the parking lot and into a warren of corridors. Before a door marked NO ENTRY, he hesitated. At last he said, "Oh, I suppose it can do no harm. If he doesn't touch anything."

Inside they found themselves in a large windowless room lit by batteries of fluorescent tubes. They cast an inhuman bluish light over equipment and worktables, a jungle of tubes and wiring, shelves crammed with flasks, beakers and notebooks.

It seemed to Eddy he stood in a magician's lair, a place outside time and space, where the world's dark secrets were created. His own dreams seemed dwarfed by comparison. He pressed closer to the men.

Dr. Newby looked up. "Eddy," he began warningly.

"Can't I help . . . or something?"

"Remember our bargain," Ronald Knowlton said. "No children allowed." He measured liquid into a beaker and thrust it into what looked like a gigantic oven. At the flick of a switch the room was filled with a humming sound. Wavering lines appeared on the viewing screen.

Eddy slumped onto a stool. Morosely he scuffed his

feet back and forth. The floor tile was an unappetizing green, irregularly splotched with brown blobs. They reminded him of the cowpies at Bosworth.

His throat tickled ominously. He cleared it. No doubt about it, it was scratchy. His head was aching too. He wondered if he had a temperature. He sighed as loudly as he dared.

This time the predatory finger found his ribs. "Thought we'd forgotten you!" Ronald Knowlton crowed. "And that candy I promised. Come along, I'll show you the machine."

Eddy trailed into the hall after him, to endure the further humiliation of having to beg change. Sullenly he accepted the coins, heaving a sigh of relief as his tormentor disappeared back into the lab. He picked out two bars, fed the machine its tribute and ate the candy slowly, leaning against the wall. He wasn't going back inside. Not with that creep still there! His father didn't want him anyway. He hadn't made a move to help him.

The candy was stale; its sweetness dried his mouth. He looked up and down the hall, but there was no water fountain to be seen. He stood there for what seemed hours. At last he let himself slide down into a sitting position, legs stuck straight out in front of him on the floor.

The corridor was warm and still. His head throbbed more and more insistently. He closed his eyes and gradually the throbbing became a dull roar, the crash of surf against a beach. It grew and grew until the air pulsated with sound.

Against his closed lids armies appeared. Men struggled, shouting and cursing as they fought and died. Horses fell too, flailing as intestines spilled from their torn bellies. The hot blood reeked in the sunlight. Their screams splintered the air. Eddy could bear it no longer; he put his hands over his ears.

But the pictures went on. Before his eyes men and horses decayed, transformed in seconds from raw flesh to grinning skeletons. Over the hideous scene the cloaked man brooded, repeating over and over: *Remember . . . remember.*

"Eddy!"

His eyes flew open. His father stood over him.

"Huh?"

"Time to go."

The corridor clock registered one-thirty. At the gate, Dr. Newby held out his hand, saying, "Well, Knowlton, you've given me a lot to think about. Let me know when you have further results."

The good-byes were completed with a minimum of cordiality. But Eddy waited till they were far down the street before he exploded. "That jerk!"

"You think so?" Something in the level tone gave pause.

He said defensively, "Well, I expected something different."

"A cross between Madame Curie and Dr. McCoy on 'Star Trek'?"

"Not some fat creep who says 'well' every second and cracks stupid jokes and—"

"Look, I wasn't crazy about him either. But that 'fat creep,' as you call him, has invented antibiotics that will save thousands of lives. Right now he's conducting research into allergies and asthma. That's why I came. To see if there was anything new that might help you."

82

"You didn't tell him about me!" Eddy protested.

"Of course! Once and for all, get it out of your head that it's something to be ashamed of!"

"But you yourself . . ." He stopped.

"What?" said his father impatiently.

He was silent. How could he admit he knew his father was ashamed of his size, his sickliness, his lack of athletic prowess?

"Another thing. I warned you. But you insisted on coming. You might at least have been polite. I was embarrassed for you."

For yourself, he thought angrily. He burst out: "Then why didn't you let me help? At least explain what you were doing. I wasn't in the way. I wouldn't have messed up. You know that!"

His father smiled a bit ruefully. "We always seem to get off on the wrong foot. I wish—"

"Yeah, I know what you wish! That I was out playing football instead of bothering you. Or—"

"That's not true, Eddy. But there's a time for daydreams and a time for action. At your age I spent my time playing ball with my friends. Not sitting on my duff fantasizing, or reading fairy tales."

"It's not just daydreams! I mean . . . I go inside my head and see things. Real things. Or pictures of them. Like at the Wax Museum." He struggled to make it plain. "Or like that day at the street market. There was a store with armor and swords, and I saw a battle. With knights and horses. I even rode with them, and there was this black knight on a black horse and—"

His father still smiled but his face had stiffened. "Sometimes you worry me, Eddy. Imagination's a fine thing.

But you have to learn to tell the difference between fact and fiction."

What was the use? In the end all their talks came to this. A fog of depression settled over Eddy.

By dinnertime his cold was worse. Eating was a pitched battle between chewing and the need to breathe. At last he pushed his plate aside.

His mother could contain herself no longer. "Are you wheezing, Eddy?"

"No!" he croaked. "And another thing. Don't call me Eddy. I'm not a kid anymore."

"What shall we call you?"

"Edward." As he said it, he wondered why it sounded silly, while on the cloaked man's lips it rang with dignity.

Kate said pertly, "How about 'King Edward'?"

A hot retort rose; he bit it back. Why was it his asthma always seemed to start a fight? What was the matter with him anyway?

He retreated early. Kate followed to take possession of the bathroom. The splash of the shower and whine of her hair dryer told him she was at her nightly ritual.

Nottingham . . . we shall not meet in Nottingham, Edward. The words returned insistently. He tried to ignore them. He didn't want to be reminded. The cloaked man was gone. In those words he had promised it.

Tomorrow they were going on to Yorkshire. Perhaps he would see Mrs. Bolton again. The thought comforted him. She at least had liked and understood him.

"What's the big idea, picking a fight like that?" Kate stood over him accusingly. Her hair clung to her cheeks in damp curls. Her eyes were indignant.

"None of your business. It's nothing to do with you."

84

"They're my parents too. And they don't need all this hassle. For your information, Mom almost canceled the trip because Dad was so tired. At his last checkup the doctor told him he had to slow down. He said he's the type that has heart attacks. Well, you know how hard he works. And after all, he's not a young man. He's sixty-one."

Frozen with shock, he stared at her. His voice shook in spite of himself. "It's not my fault."

"You're not much help."

"If she was so worried, then why did we come?"

"Oh, grow up, Eddy!" she snapped. "Just because you didn't want to. This isn't only a vacation for her. She had to come to do research for her book. Because if Dad gets sick or"—she faltered—"well, her job at the college might depend on it. She's supposed to write as well as teach. And what with taking care of you . . . us, I mean . . . she hasn't had time for writing."

"I haven't been sick much this year."

"What do you call three times in the hospital? Or had you forgotten?"

He only wished he could. He didn't like to think of those trips to the emergency room. His parents' panicky faces . . .

"Why didn't they tell me he's sick?"

"He's not exactly sick. I mean . . . it's not a crisis. He just needs some peace and quiet."

"They could have told me."

"I guess Mom thought you were too young. Besides—"

"Yeah," he growled. "With my asthma . . ."

"Don't get sore. I think they baby you too much. But now you know, you can help. Don't look so tragic. Nothing's going to happen. Really." Her face softened. "Hey, I almost forgot. Here." She handed him a booklet.

"What is it?"

"It's about the kings and queens of England. Read it. You'll find out what your precious Richard was like." She started for the door.

"Where you going?"

"To Dad and Mom's room. To play Hell's Bells. Want to come?"

He shook his head. He had to be alone. Alone to absorb the terrifying new idea that his father—his own father might— He couldn't bring himself to think it!

He flipped open the booklet. There were royal coats of arms, accounts of Anglo-Saxon kings with improbable names such as Egbert, Ethelbold, Ethelred. Grinning, he reached up and switched on the lamp. Instantly he was enveloped in a golden circle, a fairy ring of safety and warmth. A jaw-cracking yawn rose to his lips. Sighing, he hoisted himself out of the chair. It was too early to go to sleep. Cold water on his face might help. He started for the bathroom.

Yet on the boundary between lamplight and the dusk beyond, he wavered, nervous about crossing over into unknown turf. He gained the bathroom in a defiant burst of speed and slammed the door after him.

When he came out he settled back into his chair to read further. The glossy new pages stuck. He clawed at them, cursing his bitten nails. At last they yielded.

Sleep was creeping over him once more. He stifled a yawn and shook his head to clear it. Resolutely, he opened to the next page.

In the silence he was suddenly aware of every breath.

There was a roaring in his ears. For staring up at him were the eyes that had haunted his every moment—waking and sleeping—since the market. He was looking at a portrait of the cloaked man!

His body was engulfed in a wave of heat; it receded, leaving him shaking with cold. His hands felt nerveless; he could hardly hold the booklet. He steadied them and forced himself to look again.

There had been no mistake. The great dark cloak was gone; the man in the portrait was richly dressed in jewels and velvet. But the face was the face of the cloaked man.

Feverishly he scanned the print for identification. Yet even before he found them, he knew what the words would say: "Richard III (Crouchback) 1483–1485. Crowned at Westminster 6 July, 1483. Buried at Leicester."

"Leicester," he repeated. "Leicester. 'They bore Richard dead into Leicester. . . . Flung naked and bleeding over a pack horse. . . . They say the herald wept.' "

The booklet fell from his hands; he recoiled from it as from an adder. He stared wildly about but there was no help to be seen. The room was empty. Chills shook him. His teeth chattered so loudly, he was sure the whole hotel must hear.

From dark corners faces swam at him, goggle-eyed and staring. He shrank and they dwindled, collapsing into shapeless monsters, apparitions of a fun-house mirror. His thoughts were racing, dodging and twisting in an effort to escape. But at each turning, down each corridor of the imagination, he met one face. The face of the cloaked man. The face of Richard the Third.

He stumbled into the hall. Somehow he found his parents' door. From inside came a hum of voices. It was all he could do not to burst in and fling himself on them, howling for comfort.

When he knocked at last, Kate opened the door. "Hi! You're just in time for the next round. My deal."

Dr. Newby glanced at him over his glasses. He put down the journal he was reading. "You all right?"

He managed a faint grin. "Yeah. I just thought I'd keep you company." A fit of coughing racked him.

His mother leapt up. "You see, John?" she said reproachfully. "I knew you shouldn't have kept him out so long. Here, dear. Stretch out on the bed. I'll put the quilt over you."

It was enough to be there with them. Through the window he watched the twilight fade from a sky of green-gold, festooned with purple swags of cloud. His mind was empty of thought and fear alike.

Gradually he realized his father was speaking. He seemed to be reading aloud. " 'Black holes in space . . . from a dying star's gravity.' "

"Four hearts," Kate announced.

Did stars die, then? If so, what became of them? Was there such a thing as a . . . ghost star?

"Listen to this. 'Some day perhaps the universe will collapse into a black hole . . . a wormhole into another universe.' "

"Your bid again, Kate," said Margaret Newby.

His mind hung struggling over unimaginable depths. *Don't look down!* cried the voice. But it was too late. He was slipping . . . sliding . . . clawing for holds. Down . . . down . . . through that wormhole into a world where the ghost of a murdering king still walked.

He was trapped! He could see the others, even talk to them. But he could never return to their safe world. And they could neither reach nor free him.

It took all his self-control not to cry. Only the impossibility of explaining kept back the tears. What would he say? And even if they believed him, what could they do?

Later, walking back to the room, Kate seemed to sense something was wrong. She put her arm around him. He was grateful. But when he got into bed he turned his face to the wall to forestall questions.

Night passed by torturous inches. He greeted daylight with relief. The mirror as he dressed reflected a face of gray pallor. His eyes looked sunken, his cheekbones crowned with hectic fever spots. His throat was so sore it hurt to breathe, and he wheezed deep in his chest.

He was really sick this time. Unexpectedly, hope flared in him. Had he been delirious the night before? Could he only have imagined a resemblance between the cloaked man and the portrait of Richard the Third? Had it been nothing but a fever dream?

If he had dared, he would have left the booklet behind. But he could no more bring himself to abandon it than to look at it again. Holding it at arm's length, he dropped it into the suitcase finally.

He was given no time to brood. Tight-lipped with worry, his mother plied him with what seemed the whole contents of her medicine kit. The day was sunny, but she tucked a blanket around him in the car. He made no protest. Talking hurt his throat.

The trip north passed in a haze of fever. By afternoon they had left the industrial midlands behind and were in open country. The landscape here was huge and bare—

unlike the cluttered lands they had quitted. On every side moors stretched away to a rim of hills on the horizon. Lonely farms cowered down, sheltering from the scouring winds.

"It's so empty," Kate said in a small voice.

But Eddy was oddly exhilarated. He straightened, gulping great breaths of the keen air. Lovingly his eyes traced and retraced the distances. All lay open, in plain sight. No danger lurked behind hedge or bush or tree. Something—a hunger he hadn't known he felt—was satisfied by this giant earth and sky. An old refrain came to him: "Home is the sailor, home from the sea; and the hunter home from the hill." Home, that was it. It was good to be home!

He drew a sharp breath. This wasn't his home! He had never been here before. Then why did he feel this joy, this sense of homecoming?

He croaked: 'D'you ever feel like something's happened before? Like you know just what's going to come next, what it all looks like and—"

"As if, not like," his mother corrected. "Really, to listen to you no one would guess you're an English teacher's child!" She caught herself. "Anyway, of course I have. The French have a name for it—*déjà vu*, already seen. Why?"

"I just wondered." He closed his eyes, pretending to doze.

The fever was rising again. His skin felt stretched and he ached all over. When they reached the hotel in Ripon, he climbed gratefully into bed.

He had just settled back against the pillows when Kate came in.

"Whaddya want?"

"There's a letter for you. They forwarded it from the hotel in London."

"From whom?"

"How should I know?"

"Put it on the table," he ordered.

It missed his nose by inches. Kate slammed out of the room.

He tugged the pillows into a comfortable mound and spread the thin airmail sheets on his knees.

Pete's scrawl was as familiar to him as his own; their desks had been side-by-side since kindergarten. Except when the teacher separated them for whispering. Yet today he might have been reading through the wrong end of a telescope. It seemed to come from very far away.

". . . a great trip . . . the Rockies are humongous!" Frowning, he turned over the page. ". . . my parents are a pain, always arguing . . . there's this one girl . . . she's great . . . know what I mean?" He kept coming back to that: "one girl . . . know what I mean?"

No he didn't! There was no such thing as a "great" girl. Girls were nosy interfering finks. Like Kate.

He crumpled up the letter and hurled it across the room. It only made the loneliness worse. He shut his eyes, trying to picture Pete's face. But the familiar features eluded him. Nothing appeared against the closed lids. Except the cloaked man's eyes. Ghost lights! He shied at the word like a frightened colt, only to return to it compulsively. Picking at the scab until the wound beneath lay raw and open. Ghosts. Once he had scoffed at the idea. Ghosts.

Only the finicky *tick-tock . . . tick-tock . . . tick-tock* of the mantel clock broke the stillness. Maddening as the Chinese water torture. If only he could turn it off! But there was no turning off his thoughts. Unbidden they crawled from the dark cupboards of his mind.

At last he burst out: "There's no such thing as ghosts!"

Yeah? said the voice in his head. *Then who's this guy? How come he looks just like Richard the Third?*

Coincidence. Pure coincidence.

Sure . . . sure!

I'll prove it. I'll get out that damned book and . . . Too late he realized what he had said. He backtracked. *Anyway it wouldn't mean a thing. Lots of people look like someone else. . . .*

Silence. It seemed to last forever. Finally he shouted: "Okay. Okay, I'll show you."

He got out of bed and crossed to where the suitcase rested by the door. The booklet was inside the cover. He picked it up with a show of unconcern.

Hardly knowing what he did, he found himself staring at the back cover. The face he sought—and dreaded—was not there!

He forced himself to start over at the beginning. Nine pages went safely by. He began to breathe easier. Ten . . . eleven . . . twelve. . . . Hope surged in him.

He opened to page eighteen with a bravado flourish. The cloaked man's eyes—Richard's eyes—stared past him into the wastes of time.

The sound of the door opening brought him sharply about. The cloaked man seemed to fill the space. Eddy kept stepping back. Until further retreat was impossible. Pinned against the bed, he waited helplessly.

The cloaked man closed the door behind him. It had a terrifying finality. He said, "So, lad. You have come back."

"Come back?"

The man shrugged. "I have waited so long." He stared at Eddy.

In his agitation he found himself wondering what to call him. "Richard" was not to be thought of. That would mean he believed . . .

"Edward . . ."

If he did not look at him, maybe he would disappear. As if he had never been. Eddy shut his eyes. A spasm of coughing shook him. When it was over he was drenched with sweat. His eyes and nose were streaming.

In one stride the man was beside him. "You are ill! You should be abed."

"It's just a cold. My asthma." The word had slipped out. But he never mentioned his asthma! It was as if the man already knew. Had always known.

"Did you not hear? To bed with you!"

He obeyed, stifling a half-hysterical giggle. Put to bed by a ghostly nursemaid! His mother would approve.

"Sir," he began, then stopped, because his voice was unsteady.

"Forgive me. I spoke over harshly. I am not angry. How could I be? With you, of all people." Half-teasingly he went on: "Have you no better name for me than 'sir'?"

"Richard," Eddy whispered, dry-lipped.

The man seemed taken aback. He nodded slowly. "It will serve. Aye, Richard Plantagenet." His pride rang like a trumpet blast.

An answering thrill ran through Eddy's body.

"Lord of this fair realm, this England. Yet none so fair as our North Country. Eh, lad?"

It took a moment to sink in. That small word: 'our.' Linking them. As if . . .

There were voices in the hall. Kate's rose above the others. "You know, Dad . . ."

Now they were at the door! Desperately he looked about, searching for a hiding place. The cloaked man—Richard—must not be found here!

That was it. The wardrobe in the corner. He jumped out of bed and grabbed Richard's arm to drag him into concealment. Then with a strangled cry he snatched his hand away. His fingers had closed on nothing. But they smarted and burned, as if they had touched dry ice!

"Eddy!" His mother swooped down. "I thought I told you to stay in bed."

Dr. Newby said, "You were supposed to keep warm. Rest."

He waited for the storm. Reproaches. Accusations. Questions about the stranger's presence. His mind worked furiously. He could say it was a waiter. Another guest who had blundered into the wrong room.

His father started toward him. "Let's have a look at you."

He bit back a cry. Because John Newby had walked right through the cloaked man. Unnoticing. As if he were no more than a puff of smoke.

Terrified his face would betray him, he stammered: "When's supper?"

He allowed himself a sidelong glance. Richard stood in

the same spot. A small smile curved his lips but his eyes were unreadable.

Even as Eddy stared his outlines blurred, grew fuzzy and indistinct. Slowly Richard was graying, life and color leached away like paper too long underwater.

His father put a hand on his forehead. "Fever's down. I think you could have something to eat now."

"What did Pete say?" Kate asked.

"Edward . . ." It was Richard's voice. It came to him clearly from that unseen unimaginable place to which he had retreated.

"What?"

"I said, what did Pete say?" She laughed. "I knew it was from him. I was teasing you."

His father gave him a little shake. "Wake up, son. You're still groggy."

He managed to say, "I . . ." and stopped. Because Richard spoke again.

"Edward, Edward, when will you come home?"

Words telltale as skywriting. And sharp with longing.

VII

On a gray afternoon a week later, Eddy sat on an upturned crate on the shore, scuffing bare feet in the sand. He had been sitting there for some time and his feet had hollowed a deep trough. Moodily he watched as the advance and retreat of the water filled and emptied the trench over and over.

Far down the shore the others strolled, stooping every now and then to retrieve some bit of flotsam and jetsam from the tideline. Beyond them the leaden waters of the North Sea tumbled, to break in yellowish ruffles against the shore.

Occasionally his mother would pause and look back. Once she raised a hand to wave, only to let it drop again.

He made no response, but the gesture stabbed him. It was so unlike her. He knew it was his fault. But how was he to explain his preoccupation? So he remained mute. Playing possum.

He had stayed in bed all week—taking his medicine, wearing a sweater, napping in short welcome snatches of unconsciousness. Confounding predictions that ranged from strep throat to pneumonia, his cold had improved steadily. He thought his mother seemed almost disappointed. She was at her happiest when he was sick—fussing over him, holding illness at bay by her presence.

96

How could he explain? He put the question once again, as he had repeatedly in the past week. Quailing, even as he pretended unconcern for his family's perplexity and hurt. Yet how was he to explain, much less apologize, for what he himself did not understand?

Since Richard had faded out of sight in the hotel room, Eddy had whipsawed between fear and hope. Dreading and, at the same time, longing for another meeting. But Richard had not reappeared. Time hung heavy.

When his mother at last pronounced him fit, the daily tedium of sightseeing had begun again. For the most part Eddy stumbled through it, deaf and dumb as if enclosed in soundproof glass. Occasionally, staring at the moors, he was convinced he saw Richard riding there. Each time, knowing it was only his imagination, he felt the same keen disappointment, a loss so painful he had to blink back tears.

He stood up, toppling the crate in his agitation. He could still catch up with the others. Anything was better than sitting alone with his thoughts!

When his father had suggested a picnic at the bird sanctuary, Eddy had been enthusiastic. Now he wondered what he had expected. To recapture the delights of childhood summers at the shore? But there were no sand castles here, no beach umbrellas, no children squealing in fear and pleasure at the surf.

This was a desolate seascape, a bar of dunes and shingled sands tenanted only by migrant birds. Under the steely sky, land and sea flowed into one another in one unmarked plain. The only flash of life or color came from the birds. Sandpipers skittered before the incoming waters; dunlin waded the tidal pools. Overhead, herring gulls dove screaming after catch or carrion.

The air was heavy with salt and the smell of decaying sea life. Now it bore voices to him also. His family was returning. All impulse for their company died.

He turned away and pain shot through his foot. Balancing like a stork on one leg, he lifted the other to find blood dripping from a deep gash on the heel. He dropped to his knees and scrabbled in the sand to find what had cut him. He uncovered a small shell; it was gemlike, an infolded whorl of pink shading to palest cream. What creature had once inhabited the tiny palace?

The smart was subsiding and he limped down to the water to wash away the blood.

Kate ran up, panting. "Look, Eddy! A hermit crab. Like the ones we used to hunt for at the shore." She waved the little creature in his face.

Its frenzied struggles roused him to fury. "Put it down! How would you like to be picked up like that?"

"Did you think I'd hurt it?" There was disbelief in her voice. And something else. Could it be pity? He dropped his eyes.

She put her captive down. Together they watched as it burrowed for cover. Eddy glanced at the shell in his hand but it was dry now. The sheen had gone, leaving it lustreless, a lifeless fossil. He let it slip from his fingers and the incoming waters took it.

When he looked up, Kate was sitting some distance away. Her sketch pad was on her knees, her face bent over her work. What he could see of her expression was not promising.

He edged closer, searching for some way to heal the breach. As his shadow fell on the paper, she glanced up and held out the half-finished sketch.

It was of Eddy standing at the water's edge. The face was half-turned, barely indicated by a few strokes of the pencil. But the mood was dark. The lips had lost their childish curve; they were taut and somber. The eyes stared unseeing into darkness. Like Richard's.

The comparison took him by surprise; he rejected it vehemently. "That doesn't look like me!"

She gazed at the drawing, then back at him. "I dunno. I'm not good at faces. They're hard. But you're different these days. Older or something." She seemed puzzled. As if her pencil had borne independent witness to something she had not yet seen. Much less understood.

Too wary to respond but not wanting, either, to retreat into isolation, he hovered. If only they could talk the way they used to. He drew a breath. . . .

"Eddy! Kate! Time to go." And the moment was lost.

The drive back to Ripon seemed interminable, punctuated by stop after unnecessary stop. One for tea. Another to buy fruit at an open-air market. Still another to take pictures. "Isn't that church glorious in this light?" Mrs. Newby fussed at her husband's shoulder as he focused. As if anyone would ever look at the picture again! And a last exasperating delay at an antiques shop while Mrs. Newby dithered between two teapots.

By the time they reached the hotel, he was tired and cross. As they came into the lobby the desk clerk said, "Dr. Newby? A lady asked for you. Not ten minutes ago."

"Who on earth?" Mrs. Newby began.

The clerk pointed. "She's still here. Sitting by the window."

She was just as he'd remembered—alert blue eyes, lined face, long neck.

"Mrs. Bolton! How'd you find us?"

She looked smug. "Elementary, my dear Watson! Actually, I'm quite proud of my detective work. You'd said something about Ripon, so I called round to all the inns and hotels. I wasn't going to pass up seeing you again. And your family. But you've been very naughty. They tell me you've been here a week. Why didn't you call?"

His mother rescued him. "That was my fault, I'm afraid. I'd laid out a heavy sightseeing schedule. And Eddy was sick the first few days. That cut into our time."

Why had she told her? Now she would know about him. Now she would think—

"Not to worry. We've met. That's all that matters."

Talk flowed smoothly. At last Mrs. Bolton rose to go, saying, "That's settled, then. I'll expect you tomorrow for tea. At my home in Middleham."

He slept dreamlessly that night. In the morning he bounced out of bed. By the time they got under way he was bubbling over. Happiness, like bike riding, seemed to be a knack one didn't forget.

As they drove into Middleham, his mother remarked, "They say this was Richard the Third's favorite home. Quite a coincidence, isn't it? I believe his castle is still standing. Maybe there'll be time to see it after tea."

He caught one glimpse of massive walls flung up against the sky. Then he averted his eyes. He didn't want to see—or know—what waited here. Not now. Not yet.

"What a darling house!" Kate cried.

It was set back from the street, a small stone house in a garden fronted with iron pickets. In the front window a clutter of china, brass and furniture was lovingly displayed. Mrs. Bolton smiled a welcome from under the ANTIQUES sign that swung over the door.

Eddy scuttled inside as fast as any hermit crab seeking shelter. Their hostess led them through the shop into a back parlor cozily furnished in mahogany and chintz. He was aware that they sat and talked; he heard laughter and the ebb and flow of conversation. But he could not have told what they said.

The unanswered questions clamored in his brain, drowning out everything and everyone. Who was the cloaked man? Could he really be the ghost of Richard the Third? Or was he just a product of Eddy's imagination, a kind of Frankenstein monster? Had he gone crazy without knowing?

He ate steadily through tea. Ham. "Gammon," Mrs. Bolton called it. Cake. Sandwiches. Nothing filled the emptiness of fear inside him.

"Eddy!" His father sounded exasperated, as if he had been trying to get his attention.

He started. "What?"

"Mrs. Bolton was talking to you."

He looked beseechingly at her.

Behind the spectacles her eyes twinkled. "Daydreaming! I was addicted to it when I was young. How it annoyed my father! Never mind. I only said it's a shame the weather has turned nasty. I had hoped to take you through the castle after tea."

For the first time he noticed it had begun to rain.

"Some other time," his father said easily. "We'll be here a few more days."

Eddy drifted. Middleham. Favorite home of Richard the Third. Ghost. King. Murderer?

There was a flash of lighting and a clap of thunder. The lights flickered and went out.

Kate gave a startled squeak. Under the table her hand sought Eddy's. More shaken than he cared to admit, he squeezed back. As his eyes adjusted to the gloom, he saw Claudia Bolton setting out candles.

"That does it, I'm afraid. The castle is out for today."

"Never mind," said Mrs. Newby. "I'd just as soon see your antiques."

Mrs. Bolton looked delighted. "I'd love to show them off. But you mustn't feel you have to buy. You're guests."

John Newby laughed. "If not here, then somewhere else. It might as well be from a friend."

Mrs. Newby was on her feet. "Come on, kids. Let's clear."

As they went into the kitchen, Kate exclaimed: "Oh! It's just like old-fashioned kitchens."

"Kate!" reproved her mother.

"She's right," said Mrs. Bolton. "It's an old house. I came here as a bride but it was in my husband's family for generations. Both he and our son were killed in the war. After that I had no money for renovations. Nor heart," she added softly.

Kate flushed. "I'm sorry. I mean . . . I love your house. It's just that it's different. Though ours isn't exactly modern either."

Eddy set his cup down on the drainboard. The porcelain was chipped and discolored, as worn as the linoleum on the floor. Even the battered pots and pans spoke of long use.

He stared at Mrs. Bolton's back as she stood at the sink, wondering what she'd looked like when she came here. Before the war had left her to grow old alone and poor. Had she been as pretty and expectant as his mother in her college graduation picture?

She turned. "Come. We'll leave these to soak. I'm anxious to show off my treasures."

The women were soon engrossed. Eddy and his father exchanged a rueful look and settled down on a pair of hard wooden chairs to wait.

The minutes crawled, marked by the ticking of the grandfather clock in the corner. Eddy fancied it kept time to the drumming rain outside. He fidgeted, yawning, stretching, crossing and uncrossing his legs to contemplate the sole of his sneaker with rapt attention.

Kate thrust a small silver object under his nose. "Look! Mrs. Bolton says it was a ball program. Girls wore them on a bracelet like a charm." Her fingers fumbled for the catch. The front flew open to reveal a tiny pad and pencil inside. "Boys used to sign up for each dance. Isn't it darling?"

Secretly, he thought it weird. He was about to say so when he noticed Mrs. Bolton listening. She had a far-off look on her face. Somehow he knew she was daydreaming about whirling around a flower-decked dance floor in the arms of an eager young man.

Grunting something unintelligible, he went over to the window. The rain had slackened but it was almost as dark as night still.

Suddenly impatience filled him. He had to get away! It

was all he could do not to put a fist through the glass.

Then: "Edward!"

He started and looked guiltily about. The women were still engrossed with a pair of china lambs. Dr. Newby sat smoking placidly.

"Richard?" he whispered.

"What?" said Dr. Newby.

"Nothing." He pushed open the door. "I'm gonna get some air."

For a moment he wavered, remembering another doorway through which he had gone out into a storm. He thrust the memory aside and started to walk, following the unfamiliar streets unhesitatingly. As if he had walked them all his life. Nothing and no one behind him. Only someone ahead. Someone he went to meet.

Gray houses. Gray cobbled streets. Gray under an iron sky and a wind that stung the eyes.

He started up an incline. In a little square ahead stood a stone pylon with a statue on top. He squinted at it through the blur of moisture, but years of wind and weather had reduced it to a lump. Misshapen. Unrecognizable.

Then, as if impelled, he raised his eyes. The castle crouched like some primeval dragon ready to spring. Lifeless yet still menacing. Its sawtoothed walls and towers dominated the landscape. He stared and stared. As if he could not get his fill.

With no conscious decision his legs carried him over the intervening space. For a moment he knew terror. As swiftly it was gone, leaving only an enormous impatience.

He crossed the drawbridge and ducked under the portcullis, flinging his arms up to protect him from the iron jaws. The sentry chamber as he passed was empty, yet he quickened his step, fearing challenge.

Now he was in the inner courtyard. Directly ahead rose the keep, a stone structure several stories high, its thick walls slotted with narrow windows.

He stopped abruptly. It was quiet here. Too quiet. In front of him a flight of steps led up to the keep door. He began to climb, slipping on the moss that clung to the worn stone.

To his astonishment the door opened easily. Inside the silence was absolute, like thick velvet. Even the persistent patter of rain could not penetrate the thick walls. He cocked his head, alert for the slightest sound, but there was nothing. At last he could bear it no longer. He flung back his head: "Hello . . . oo."

Two birds hurtled down from somewhere high above. Chattering and scolding, they circled until, with a last indignant flirt of their tail feathers, they regained their unseen roost.

He grinned and ventured a few steps further, looking curiously around. He was in an immense hall. In its center a fire crackled in an open hearth. The smoke curled upward into the rafters above.

Then he heard a tiny sound, the whisper of indrawn breath. He spun about. Richard stood beside him, a Richard he had never seen before. As in the portrait the cloak was gone, and with it the tension of the wiry frame. In their place was a kingly Richard dressed from head to toe in crimson. His tunic was embroidered with golden thread; a great jewel hung on his breast. It caught the firelight, winking and sparkling like a cat's eyes in the dark.

Bright as it was, Richard's eyes were brighter. His lips curved up in a triumphant smile.

Seeing it, Eddy was afraid again. Was this the smile of the hunter who has stalked and cornered his prey?

"You have come home at last, Edward!"

Home is the hunter . . .

"Come!"

He followed helplessly. Their footsteps rustled in the rushes covering the floor.

At the far end of the hall a table stood on a raised platform. It was laid for a meal, with trenchers, platters and tankards at each place. In the center stood a great bowl of apples. Their tang mingled with the tantalizing smell of meat roasting; try as he would, Eddy could not see where it came from.

"See, Edward, the rising sun of York."

His eyes followed the imperious finger. On the wall behind the table hung a banner emblazoned with a golden sun. He looked at it without surprise, as if he had seen it often.

He hung back, groping for questions, but Richard gave him no chance to speak. Without touch, without command, with nothing but the force of his will he herded him on. Along winding corridors lit by torches that flamed in their brackets on the walls. Up endless flights of steps and down again. Through rooms of every kind. Guardrooms and armories. Reception chambers. Bedchambers furnished with chests and wooden bedsteads heaped with furs to keep out the drafts that seemed to penetrate every cranny and chink in the walls. Eddy shivered.

And everywhere was that dreamlike sense of life, of

habitation. A familiarity so strong he could almost taste it. The unseen people who lived and worked here were people he knew. Or would have if they had shown themselves. If he could just remember.

In one room, Richard lingered. It was richly furnished, the walls hung with tapestries. On the bed were strewn clothes—a silk gown, a velvet cloak lined with fur. In one corner stood boots, mud-encrusted as if the owner had just stepped out of them. And on a small table there were trinkets—an ivory-backed mirror, a comb, bits of jewelry.

Eddy's heart thudded painfully. He looked around for the owner of this finery. Surely she was close-by. He could smell her fragrance still, faint but hauntingly familiar. Odd. Because his mother never wore perfume. And Kate went in for stronger stuff. Yet he could swear he had smelled this scent before.

He glanced at Richard. His head was up, sniffing the air like an animal. So it wasn't just his imagination. There was something . . . someone here.

Was that the whisper of long skirts sweeping the floor? He took an involuntary step forward. If he could just touch something—anything—maybe he would know. Maybe he would remember, even see her.

He stopped short. What if the icy cold he'd felt when he touched Richard clung to these remains? What if they crumbled under his hand? *Step on a crack, break your mother's back!*

Richard's eyes were on him, fixed in mute appeal. He wrenched his own away. There was no triumph in it, only the sour sense of failure he so often felt with his father. What was it? Oh, what had he done?

Richard turned away, shoulders sagging. Eddy followed hopelessly. And then Richard began to speak. Words poured from him, a flood tide of recollection by turns joyous and wistful, as if the dams of memory had been swept away. People, events, the daily life of castle and realm. Talk punctuated by "remember" and "but you know that" and "you ever loved that." Words that took for granted a shared past. A past dead some five hundred years.

Was it one hour or two or three before they came again into the courtyard? The rain had churned the grass and dirt into a quagmire. Rain and something else.

"Hoofprints!" Eddy said incredulously.

Richard shook his head in mock reproof. "The stables are but yonder. Had you forgotten?" He smiled. "And you were ever to be found there. Or in the kennels with the hounds. When you might better have been at your lessons." His smile took the sting out of the words.

Eddy found himself smiling back. They had been good days! Perhaps . . . Over the sighing of the wind he thought he heard a sound. Was it a horse neighing? But the stables were empty. Had been for years. Like the castle itself. Though there was food, clothes, fire. People?

He stepped back. Richard followed, hands outstretched. In supplication or menace? Yet Richard still smiled.

Again he heard the words: *I have killed you twice already!* Had they been Richard's or John Newby's? What was it they wanted of him?

He turned to run. Even as part of him longed to throw himself on Richard. If only for the terrible and wonderful relief of giving up the flight!

With a smothered sob, he ran. Through the courtyard pocked with ghostly hoofprints. Under the portcullis jaws. Past the empty sentry chamber. Across the draw-bridge, through the square and down the cobbled hill.

At the corner he paused. Against his will he looked back. There was no one following. But through the mist and rain, the castle brooded. A fossil frozen in time.

VIII

When he stumbled back into Mrs. Bolton's house—wet, tired and resigned to a scolding for his long absence—he found her arranging for Kate and him to go pony-trekking the next day.

He could only marvel at her offhand veto of his mother's plans. "York's all very well for you," she said firmly, "but these children need fresh air and exercise. I'm sure my friend can manage horses and a guide. I'll go call him."

Silently he guffawed at Kate's face on hearing herself classified as a child.

The next morning was still overcast and cold. Bridles and saddle leather squeaked stiffly, and the ponies, skittish in the keen air, danced about snorting clouds of condensed breath. Their hooves struck the cobbles of the stableyard with a frosty clang.

Eddy pulled his windbreaker collar up around his chin. Only to make a wild grab for the reins as his pony, taking advantage of his inattention, lunged for the watering trough. Automatically Eddy tightened his knees and hauled in on the reins. The pony's ears twitched; it craned its neck around to peer at its rider. Unexpectedly it bared yellow teeth and nipped at Eddy's toes.

"Hey! Stop that. Don't do that!"

Colin, their guide, grinned and ambled over to jerk the pony's head away.

110

"None o' that now! Heads oop," he commanded in his rich Yorkshire voice.

He moved to Kate's side. For some time she and her mount had been engaged in a unequal contest. Whenever she got a foot in the near stirrup and prepared to throw the other leg over, the mare danced just out of reach. Now Colin gathered the reins into his own hand and slapped the fat gray rump. The pony nuzzled him, a picture of injured innocence.

Kate was close to tears. "Oh, just go on without me," she quavered. "I'll never be able to do it."

Colin shook his head. Under his reproving eye she reddened, then hoisted herself into the saddle. She perched there rigid with fright, clutching the reins so hard her knuckles gleamed.

From where she leaned against the fence, Mrs. Bolton called: "You've the makings of a rider, Edward. A good natural seat and hands."

In an excess of confidence he kicked the pony forward. It had long since taken his measure and balked, heaving a reproachful sigh. Eddy flushed and stole a look about, hoping no one had noticed.

Mrs. Bolton laughed. "Cantankerous little beasts, aren't they? Never mind. It'll go when Colin's does. They're trained to follow the leader."

Finally Colin mounted and led the way slowly out into the lane.

Eddy was concentrating so hard on keeping his seat that he paid scant attention to his surroundings at first. But gradually he relaxed and began to enjoy the world from this novel elevation.

Their road lay between low stone walls. The fields

beyond were hazed with morning mist. Looking back, Eddy could barely make out the outlines of farmhouse and stables. A pale sun fought to break through the clouds; as yet it shed scant warmth. Eddy shivered, regretting the sweater he had left behind in the tack room.

Colin's horse broke into a trot and the others followed. Eddy jounced uncomfortably, then his body settled to the rhythm. Colin looked back, nodding his approval.

Kate still flopped about, grunting with pain at every step. Both feet had come out of the stirrups. She threw Eddy an anguished look. "Whoa, darned horse! Walk. Walk, I say!" Despairingly she dropped the reins and threw her arms around the pony's neck.

"Trouble?" Colin grinned broadly. "I'm afraid these ponies speak nought but Yorkshire."

She looked so comical, clinging on for dear life, that Eddy laughed. Unguided, her pony ambled to the roadside and stopped, stretching its neck to crop the grass beyond the wall.

"Uh-uh!" Colin warned. "Mustn't let her do that. Else she'll eat her way across the countryside."

Between fright and embarrassment, Kate was red as a beet. Somehow she managed to retrieve the reins and pull up. The mare just flicked its tail as if to dislodge a fly. Kate tugged again. This time the pony laid its ears back and kicked.

Kate screamed.

"She's a fly one," Colin said. "I'd best lead you for a bit. You'll see. She'll give me no trouble."

"Fly?" Eddy inquired.

"Tricky. Horses are like people. They take advantage if they can."

112

They started off at a more sedate pace. A mile or so further on, Colin led them through a gap in the wall to strike off uphill onto the moor. Despite the thick cover of gorse and heather, the ground was stony and the ponies' hooves dislodged a steady shower of pebbles. Eddy stiffened, fearful of a stumble. But the beasts picked their way with assurance.

Kate turned to smile at him.

Eddy smiled back. "Better?"

"Much."

At the crest of the hill, Colin called a halt. The ponies blew gustily.

Below and to the south lay Middleham, a tiny patch of habitation in the ocean of moorlands. Eddy's breath caught as he picked out the castle. Was Richard still there?

Kate followed his look. "Romantic, isn't it?"

"That shows all you know! Castles were built for war. Not love." He drew the word out contemptuously.

"Just wait till you're older!"

Colin broke in. "We'd best get on. We've a way to go before we stop for lunch."

He led them downhill until they reached a rutted track tucked deep in the fold between two fells.

"The farmers hereabouts use it on market day," Colin said. He eyed them hopefully. "It's a grand place for a canter."

"Great!" Eddy said, with more enthusiasm than he felt.

Kate protested: "Oh, but . . ."

"Come on," Colin urged. "It's easier than trotting."

Grimly she took back the reins, tucked in her hair, and adjusted her feet in the stirrups. "Ready," she announced through clenched teeth.

Colin shortened rein, laid his hands low on the horse's neck and kicked him. The roan needed no urging. It stretched out its legs and ran, clods of dirt hurtling behind its flying heels.

Kate's mare followed. There were barely time for Eddy to hope she wouldn't fall off before his own mount fled down the trail in hot pursuit.

The wind stung his face. Trees, boulders and bushes ran together in a blur of speed. He was aware of sheep, puffs of white that dotted the hillsides and scattered, bleating, as he thundered by. He felt an instant's sharp regret that Richard was not there to see him. Then there was nothing in the world but speed and motion, borne along on the rushing air.

The track veered and his pony swerved, carrying him under a low branch. Instinctively he ducked and shut his eyes. When he opened them again his horse was standing in a copse beside a stream. Kate and Colin had dismounted.

He swung his legs over and slid off. His knees buckled under him; he grabbed for the saddle and hung on till his legs steadied.

Colin chuckled. "Stiff? That's nothing to what you'll be tomorrow!"

Unembarrassed, Eddy grinned back. Nothing could upset him, not after that ride! If only the day would never end.

Tottering slightly, he led the pony over and tied it beside the others, copying Colin's knots as best he could. His fingers felt clumsy and unpracticed on the leather.

Then he slumped down on the turf beside the stream. In spite of the cold his shirt was wet with sweat. Impulsively he wriggled out of his jacket and stripped off his shoes and socks to plunge both feet into the swift brown water. Gasping he pulled them out again.

"Why didn't you tell me it's so cold?" he spluttered.

Colin was retrieving the lunches from the saddlebags. "You didn't ask," he replied.

Kate unzipped her jacket and laid it down, setting out the lunches on it as if it were a banquet cloth.

"You'll take cold," Colin protested.

"I don't like ants in my food!"

Colin paid no attention to her rudeness. He kept stealing looks at her. She seemed not to notice, but soon she fished out a comb and set her tumbled hair to rights. Eddy saw she took care to sit where the sun fell full on her coppery head.

He said loudly, "Why do you call them ponies?"

"We call anything under fourteen and a half hands a pony. A small horse, really."

Kate edged closer to him. She said sweetly, "After all, Eddy, out west they call them cow-ponies."

Miss Know-it all! He picked up his lunch and stumped off upstream to eat by himself.

She was nothing but a showoff. And what did she have to show off about? Not her riding. That was for sure! She might be a hotshot basketball star, but as a rider she was pathetic.

He was going to be a great rider! Or die in the attempt. Though after he went home he'd probably never get another chance.

Anyway, he was onto her. She couldn't impress Colin with her riding, so she'd gone all soft and cutesy. And Colin had fallen for it. Hook, line and sinker. It was nothing new. He'd seen it all before. The trouble was, this time it wasn't just Colin, but Pete too. Pete, the friend he had counted on. Pete, with his: "one girl . . . she's great . . . know what I mean?" He felt suddenly as if everyone else in the world had been picked for some team. To play a game he didn't know and didn't want to. Odd man out!

The scrape of hooves on rock recalled him. He looked up. On the far bank of the stream a horse and rider stood quietly; the rider's cloak stirred in the breeze.

Suddenly Eddy was aware of every sound—the clatter of water over stone, the snorts of the ponies in the copse behind him, bird song.

Richard was still. Only the tension of his hands betrayed his efforts to control the great horse. His boots were flecked with mud, the horse's flanks lathered. It came to Eddy they had ridden hard and far to keep this rendezvous.

Without warning, they clattered across the stream. Beside Eddy, Richard reined in so sharply the horse reared and danced, pawing the air.

Eddy scrambled up in alarm.

"Why did you run away yesterday?"

The question took him by surprise. He stammered: "I don't know. I mean . . . it was weird somehow. At the castle."

Richard seemed puzzled. "Weird?"

"Strange. I mean . . . I felt like I knew the place. Like I'd been there before. All those things. The fire and the food and stuff. The people . . ." He faltered.

Richard cut him short. "We must return."

"To the castle?"

There was no reply.

He stalled for time. "How would we get there?"

"My horse can carry both of us. He has before."

Indignantly, Eddy said, "I've got my own. Behind those trees."

"Fetch him, then."

"But—"

With one sinuous movement Richard dismounted. Eddy recoiled.

"Afraid still, Edward? And of me?"

Before his stricken look, Eddy went cold. He tried to think of something to say.

It was too late. Wordlessly Richard swung into the saddle again. He wheeled the gray and put spurs to his sides. They cleared the stream in one leap and galloped up the hillside. At the crest he reined in for an instant. Then horse and rider disappeared, leaving the green rise empty and still.

For a moment Eddy was frozen. Then he splashed across the stream in pursuit. One short breathless climb—and he was on the hilltop. But on the wide landscape nothing moved; no living thing was to be seen except the sheep.

At last he roused himself and went to rejoin the others. Kate and Colin still sat side by side where he had left them. Colin looked bemused. Kate's head tilted slightly toward him, as if it were too heavy for her to hold upright.

"Did you see a man on a gray horse go by?" he demanded.

"There's been no one at all."

He said abruptly, "I'm sick of this place. Can I start back?"

Colin looked doubtful. "If you should lose your way . . ."

"I won't. I've got a good sense of direction. Even my dad says so."

Kate came to his rescue. He had a hunch it was only to ensure more time alone with Colin.

"Let him. He rode beautifully. Better than me."

"That's a fact!"

She looked taken aback but continued gamely: "He never gets lost. He found his way all over London by himself."

"And that's more than I could do! Too many people by half. All right, lad. Tighten up Gaffer's cinch and let's see you mount up."

Eddy sidled over to the pony, eyeing him nervously. "Good boy," he said, "there's a good boy. I won't hurt you. Stand still, Gaffer. Good boy!"

The little bay flicked its tail as Eddy tugged at the cinch. When it was as tight as it would get, he took up the reins, put his foot in the stirrup, and grabbed the saddle to hoist himself up. At that instant Gaffer exhaled, a long gusty sigh like air flowing from a punctured tire. The saddle slid down over the deflating flank and came to rest amidships at a drunken angle.

Colin laughed. "That's the oldest trick of all. This time tighten up before he breathes in."

Red-faced, Eddy secured the balky strap again. Once more he shortened rein and this time got into the saddle without mishap.

"Good lad. You'll make a rider yet. Now, take the track back two or three miles to the cutoff. It'll be on your left. And remember, the trail climbs before it goes back down to the road. You can't go wrong."

Eddy hardly listened. He was in a fever to be off. To find out—if he could—where Richard had gone.

"We'll be along soon," Colin went on. "Likely catch up before you know it."

For a time Eddy could almost forget where he was going. In the broad waste of moor there was nothing and no one but him and the horse, joined in the intoxication of power.

"If I could only stay and ride forever."

At the sound of his voice, the pony slowed and bent to graze. Eddy grinned and shortened rein. "Oh, no, you don't!"

They continued so for some distance. Suddenly Eddy shivered. The air was colder now, the sun withdrawn into a slatey sky. To his dismay the track was obscured by mist, not the haze of morning but a thick blinding blanket.

Better get outta here, he thought. "Get up, boy!"

But the fog came on with terrifying speed. Soon he could see only a few feet ahead. Alarmed, he drew up to consider his next move.

Should he try to go back? Colin would know the way. But the mist behind was, if anything, denser than that ahead. Nothing for it but to go on!

Momentarily, the obscurity lifted. To his relief, he thought he could make out the cutoff. He strained to see. Was it the right one? It was hard to tell. If only he'd paid attention to Colin's directions!

He reined left and started uphill. He had thought the fog would lessen as they climbed, but it mocked his hopes. It was as cottony and smothering as a cloud bank.

Close by he heard a plaintive baa . . . aa. . . aa. Soon a woolly face loomed in his path.

"Move over!"

The face peered stupidly and bleated again. It was then that he saw the lamb just behind and under its mother—legs buckled, head butting at her in the urgency of suckling.

"Sorry," he apologized. "I guess you can't move at that."

Gaffer was already picking his way around the obstacle. Eddy laughed softly. There was something reassuring about the baby's single-minded pursuit of dinner.

Gradually the ground leveled off. He guessed they had reached the ridgeline.

The mist pressed in from all sides, a stifling clinging cloud. The sharp consciousness of danger tugged at him, a danger somehow associated with the moor and fog. More terrible than merely losing his way.

Then it came to him! The mire in the Sherlock Holmes story. The Great Grimpen Mire. A bottomless oozy pit that swallowed people, ponies, hounds without warning. Without trace. A black hole!

It would be so easy to blunder into it. Fatally easy. He could feel the slime rising, covering his mouth, his nostrils. Rising till his eyes bulged with the suffocating pressure.

Out of the fog ahead a shape materialized. Gaffer shied and Eddy cried out. He struggled to stay in the saddle. Cold sweat poured off him. He fought to ward off panic.

The shape resolved itself; Richard said accusingly, "You are lost, boy!" His anger was somehow reassuring.

"It came on so fast."

"It is often so with the sea fret."

"Sea fret?"

"So we call it here in the North Country. It comes from the sea. Had you forgotten? No matter. You did right to find me. I will guide you home." He beckoned for Eddy to follow.

"Sir . . . the others . . ."

"What others?"

"Kate and Colin." And as Richard still hesitated, he said again, "Please! I left them back by the stream. They were going to follow me but they may have lost their way."

Richard shook his head. "Tsch! the moor is no place for children in the mist. There are cliffs. Mires. The fault is not yours, though. I should not have left you."

So the vision had been true—the sucking mud, oblivion. Looking into the blankness ahead, Eddy quailed.

"Are you sure you know the way?"

"I spent the best years of my childhood on this moor." As they rode slowly downhill Richard called: "Stay close."

They made slow but steady progress. Every so often Richard paused, cocking his head slightly as if listening.

For what, Eddy did not know. He himself heard nothing. But he followed confidently. Soon he lost all sense of time and place.

When at last it seemed he could bear the strain no longer, he found they were on level ground again. The going was easier here, and the horses picked up their heads and stepped out briskly.

Suddenly Eddy caught the sound of voices. He cupped his hand behind his ear to listen. The sound came again. He slumped in the saddle with relief.

Two shapes appeared. Colin was in the lead, holding Kate's reins. Behind him Kate was white with worry, but she greeted Eddy joyfully.

"Thank God we've found you!"

Colin's grin split his face like a jack-o'-lantern. "More like he found us! Were you lost, lad? Is that why you came back?"

"No. We . . . I came back to find you." He looked nervously about but Richard was nowhere to be seen.

"Well, if you're not the cool one!" He drew closer and slapped Eddy on the shoulder. "Well done, lad!"

Their return across the all but invisible land was uneventful. For Eddy it held the air of unreality. Colin led now, but always in the mist Eddy was aware of another guide. He found the unseen presence comforting.

If seemed hours before Gaffer's hooves struck a paved surface. Startled, Eddy looked up. The mist was thinning. Ahead, he knew, lay the haven of farmhouse and stables.

Richard murmured: "I must leave you now, Edward."

"But I . . . you wanted me to come back."

A half-smile softened Richard's face. "Never fear, lad. We shall meet again."

The great horse gathered itself and sailed effortlessly across the wall. Horse and rider were soon lost from sight. A small shower of stones rattling down the hill marked their passage.

Mrs. Bolton and the Newbys were huddled by the paddock rail as the ponies plodded into the yard. They must have been standing for some time. Mrs. Newby's face was white and pinched, and Dr. Newby was slapping his hands together to keep them warm.

"Thank God!" cried Mrs. Bolton. "We were about to organize a search party. This is the worst I've seen in years."

"Come up fast," Colin agreed.

Anxious to show off his knowledge, Eddy said, "It's often that way with the sea fret."

Colin's stare told him he had blundered. "It's a wonder how you've picked up our talk. You sure you've never been here before?"

To avoid explanations, he slid down and ran to help Kate. She staggered on her feet, and Mrs. Newby flew to her side.

She shook them off. "I'm okay. You should have seen Eddy! You'd think he'd been riding all his life. He was a real hero too. He came back for us in all that fog."

Inwardly, he groaned. Now the fat was in the fire! They would want to know how the group had gotten separated. Why he had gone on ahead. And, as usual, he would be blamed.

A hand fell on his shoulder. He looked up into his father's face.

"Dad, I . . ."

Dr. Newby smiled. "Forget it, son. I'm proud of you.

And grateful that everything turned out all right. Also that you liked the riding. Because Mrs. Bolton has invited you to stay on and visit for a couple of weeks while the rest of us go to Scotland. We can pick you up on our way south. How about it?"

He was speechless; his eyes met Mrs. Bolton's. Grinning, she said, "It will be wonderful to have someone young about the house again. And Colin's father has agreed to let you help out in the stables in return for the chance to ride every day."

Now he found his voice. "Can I ride Gaffer?"

Colin paused in the stable door. "You seem to suit each other well enough. And it'll be grand to have the help."

"That's settled, then," said Mrs. Bolton. "I'll expect you first thing tomorrow morning." Her hand touched Eddy's. "Remember our talk in London? Perhaps you'll find what you've been looking for here in the North Country!"

IX

Sitting in Mrs. Bolton's sunny kitchen the next morning, Eddy still could hardly believe in his good fortune. A short time before, his family had deposited him, bag and baggage, at her door. His hostess had greeted his scant possessions with approval: "Good lad! I see you travel light."

There had been one bad moment when he overheard his mother, in that sickroom voice that set his teeth on edge, warning Mrs. Bolton about his asthma. He had panicked, sure that now she would change her mind and take back the invitation.

But she'd passed it off lightly. And his family had driven away amidst the usual flurry of last-minute instructions to "keep warm," "keep dry," and "be sure and help around the house." His father had been silent. As so often, Eddy wondered what he was really thinking.

They were to pick him up on their return from the western highlands. Meanwhile, he was free! Free for two whole weeks to work in the stables, ride with Colin and explore the North Country. "Our North Country," Richard called it. A chill ran through him. He must have been crazy to let himself in for two weeks in Richard's stronghold!

Mrs. Bolton got up and scraped the last of the eggs onto his plate. "Don't think I've forgotten what it is to feed a growing boy!" Her face was alight with excitement. If anything she seemed more thrilled than he. He relaxed. It was going to be all right. More than all right!

With a sigh of pleasure he reached for the toast. It crunched agreeably; butter spurted down his chin. If he hadn't been so sore from riding, he would have pinched himself to make sure he wasn't dreaming.

His hostess carried the plates to the sink. She threw open the window, admitting a blast of frigid air that seemed sure to shrivel the geraniums on the sill.

"Stupendous!" she exclaimed, breathing deeply. "Simply stupendous. I've never seen such a summer. You must have brought the heat with you from London."

"Heat?" Eddy twined chilled fingers around his cocoa mug, grateful for the warmth.

"Oh, I suppose by your standards this isn't hot at all. But hereabouts, one sunny day a heat wave makes!" She beckoned him to the door. "Come along. I'll show you your room and you can unpack. You don't want to be late your first day of work."

He pocketed the last of the bacon and followed. The hall was dark, the stairs narrow and steep. But Claudia Bolton took them lightly.

"It must be a very old house," he said.

"As I told you, it was in my husband's family for years."

"Were they knights?"

She laughed. "Hardly. Why do you ask?"

He hesitated. "Well . . . because of the castle. I mean . . . I wondered if they were here in Richard's time."

She did not answer. Pushing open a door at the end of the upstairs hall, she said, "This is your room, Edward. For as long as you care to stay."

It was tiny and slightly askew. A whitewashed cubbyhole with slanting floor tucked under the eaves. Even the window was crooked, an off-center octagon fitted with thick bubbly panes of glass. The old nursery rhyme about the "crooked house" came into his mind.

"It was Ian's. My son, that is. He grew so tall he couldn't stand upright in it. He was forever hitting his head on the lintel when he walked in. George—my husband—tacked a pillow to it. Said he couldn't be bothered to bandage the cuts and bruises. Of course, it's no problem to you! And you'll love the view of the moor from the window. As he did."

Avoiding her eye he looked curiously about, mentally cataloging the pine chest and rush-bottom chair, the bed spread with a faded red quilt. A small bookshelf heaped with dusty books stood in the window alcove. Nothing else. No pictures. No rug to warm the bare floor. The room of a young man long dead. A room with an empty waiting look. Haunted. Like the castle.

He had been quiet too long. She said anxiously, "It's all right, isn't it? Not too small?" As if, seeing it through his eyes, for the first time she noticed the bleakness.

He forced a smile. "It's great. Really. Just great."

"That's settled then. Now, let's get you unpacked. I promised Colin I'd have you there first thing. They have their hands full this time of year, what with the pony-trekkers and racehorses."

"Racehorses?"

"Middleham's a center for Thoroughbreds. Didn't you know? But not to worry. You won't have anything to do with them. You're to help out with the ponies. All it takes is stout legs and a strong back."

He grimaced. Muscles he hadn't ever heard of were groaning and protesting down his back and legs.

He planted himself between Mrs. Bolton and the suitcase as he emptied it, managing to smuggle the statue into a drawer unseen. The precaution proved unneccessary; she seemed unconcerned with his possessions. His mother would have hovered; he marveled at the contrast.

The days that followed left no time to ponder adult vagaries. Never in his life had he worked so hard. Mrs. Bolton drove him to the stables each morning before opening her shop. The first part of the day was spent mucking out stalls, spreading fresh straw, distributing feed and water and currying the ponies. Then came the never-ending chore of mending and cleaning tack. Back-breaking work, yet he came to love the sight and smell and feel of everything connected with the horses. Even the pungent smell of dung.

He learned to walk boldly up to the most evil-tempered animal—to groom it, even to pick its feet up and dislodge the dirt and stones lodged in the hooves.

Best of all were the afternoons when, in turn with Colin and the other hands, he exercised his charges. And when Colin pronounced himself satisfied with his riding, he was allowed to shepherd tourist parties onto the moor.

He came to know the ponies as friends, with all their foibles and crochets. The little mare Kate had ridden was ever alert to inexperienced riders. It would stop dead before the slightest rise, sighing as if to say, "You expect me to climb that mountain with this deadweight on my back?" And Colin or he would have to jerk the reins and slap its rump to start it up again.

But it was Gaffer, the spoiled bay of his first ride, that came to have the deepest hold on him. Eddy took to hoarding bits of apple and sugar cubes. At the sight of him, the pony would nicker and trot over to pin him against the fence as it searched his pockets with greedy velvet lips. Eddy had to grit his teeth to curb his jealousy when some uncaring tourist rode out on the animal he'd come to count his own. He thought he hid his feelings until the day Colin said, "You'll miss the little beast when you go home. More than it'll miss you, likely!" Eddy flushed and for once found no ready answer.

Usually Mrs. Bolton picked him up just after six. He learned to recognize and welcome the erratic *chug-a-ta-chug* of her old "Mini-Minor" as it labored up the lane. For the first few nights he dragged himself upstairs right after dinner to fall into an exhausted sleep. But aching limbs and callused palms soon became badges of honor, symbols of a newfound competence and strength. And the evenings settled into a companionable routine.

Mrs. Bolton taught him to play chess, saying, "Haven't had anyone to play with in ages. You'll be good at it. As you are with the horses. Colin and his father are delighted."

Often, though, they simply talked the evenings away before the fire. Now when he tumbled into bed, the little room seemed to him a haven—more truly his own than that other room so many miles away across the Atlantic.

By the middle of the second week, he felt as if he'd lived there always. Not with that sixth sense that had led him through the streets the first day, but with the certainty of belonging to a place he'd made his own. Now home, school, friends and family no longer seemed quite real to him. Even Richard had faded a little. He had not shown himself again. Yet in the few quiet moments he found himself watching and waiting for him. Because without

Richard, Middleham was not home after all. The thought was disturbing, and Eddy pushed it out of his mind.

One evening, with Mrs. Bolton out on business of her own, Eddy ventured into the castle grounds again. Richard was not there, as Eddy had somehow known he would not be. Yet when he went into the great hall of the keep, he was again conscious of human presence. This time he was comforted by it. The unseen beings were friends. His friends. And he himself was no intruder but part of the castle's life. As Richard was.

But his day-to-day realities were the huge sky and the moor—burnished by the summer sun, washed clean by fierce rains. Above all, there was the warmth of Gaffer's body against his, responsive to the lightest touch of hand or knee. These satisfied him as nothing in his life before.

One evening he burst out: "I don't want to go home. Not ever. I want to stay. I love it, all of it. The ponies, the stables, this house, the North Country." Then, faltering, because it was hard to say: "Being with you. I mean . . . you're my friend." It was the closest he could bring himself to telling her he loved her.

Mrs. Bolton said nothing for a moment. Then: "Perhaps they'll send you back next summer. I'd love that!" She sounded wistful, and he was sorry he had spoken. Her tone bore witness to a loneliness he hadn't dreamed of. Adults always seemed complete to him, self-sufficient. If they too could feel helpless and alone, then there was no such thing as safety. Not anywhere!

He overslept the next day, and they made a late and hurried start. To his amazement, he found Colin, usually long since hard at work, sitting on a stool beside the stable door. His ruddy face was glum.

130

"What's up?"

"Slipped on a cobble last night and sprained my ankle." Colin indicated the crutches propped against the doorframe. "Father and t'other lads took the ponies to the county fair. First one I've missed in years." He sounded very sorry for himself.

Eddy swallowed hard. "Bad luck. For me, too. I guess that means no riding today. And I'm leaving day after tomorrow." He turned away, struggling to master his disappointment.

Unexpectedly Colin chuckled. "Come with me, lad." Grabbing up his crutches, he led the way into the stables, swinging along the aisle between the stalls with surprising agility.

"I'd not forgotten you're leaving us. I told Father Gaffer'd gone lame and couldn't be shown. He's yours for the day. T'other chores can wait."

Speechless with joy, Eddy could only squeeze Colin's hand. Then he raced for the tack room.

Moments later, with Gaffer bridled and saddled, he clattered through the yard and took the shortcut behind the farm, up the hillside and onto the moor. Once in the open, he kicked Gaffer into a gallop. With the wind racing by and the thud of hoofbeats in his ears, he could forget the enchantment was about to end, forget everything and everyone except the joy of the golden moment.

Just ahead lay a low wall. Before Eddy had time to think, Gaffer hurled himself up and over. Then he stretched out his legs and ran as if to the world's end.

Beside himself, Eddy shouted: "We did it, Gaffer! Oh, good boy. We did it!"

Presently he pulled the speeding pony up and slid from

his back. Gaffer dropped his head and grazed, sides heaving, chest and flanks dark with sweat.

Eddy leaned against him, reins held loosely in one hand. He thought fiercely that he had to savor—no, devour—this day! To hold and keep it safe against the gray sameness of life. A life to which he would soon return.

"Why?" he whispered. "Why do I have to go back? I want to stay. I belong here. I wish . . . oh, I wish . . ."

Overhead, a winged shape hovered. Seemingly weightless, it drifted light as thistledown against the tender blue. He gazed up at it, spellbound.

Without warning it plummeted earthward. As it fell, there came a shrill metallic keening. Eddy's heart jolted. Had it been shot?

In a confused impulse at rescue, he began to run. But the rough ground slowed him. He found himself saying over and over, "No! Oh, no!"

Gaffer trotted obediently in his wake. Eddy stopped short. Of all the idiots! Running when he had the horse.

He scrambled back into the saddle. At that instant the fallen bird catapulted upward from the grass at Gaffer's feet and raked away west in a burst of speed.

He was still staring after it when he heard hoofbeats. He turned to see Richard on the big gray.

"How like you the falcon's flight?" The pointing hand was gauntleted.

"Is that what it was? I've never seen one before."

Richard looked puzzled. There was a brief silence. Then he shrugged. "Aye, a falcon. Well manned too. Look, you." From a pouch at his belt he drew a feathered bundle like a small bird. It was attached to a long furled cord.

Richard twirled the cord expertly, whirling it overhead until the dummy swooped and soared in simulated flight. At the same instant he cried out.

The falcon must have seen and responded instantaneously. It circled downward, quartering the sky in descending segments. At last it dropped onto Richard's wrist, digging sharp talons into the gauntlet.

Richard bent over it. His fingers moved caressingly on the black-capped head, then dropped to ruffle the breast where the feathers shaded from fawn to pink. The falcon bobbed with pleasure, chortling deep in its throat like a stroked cat.

"He's beautiful!" Eddy exclaimed.

"She." Richard smiled at his surprise. "The female is the deadlier hunter. Her name is Jezebel."

"I guess it's the same as with lions. My teacher told us the female hunts for the pride."

Jezebel stared unwinkingly. Her eyes were piercing, their dark centers ringed with an inhuman yellow. Under their gaze Eddy shifted uncomfortably.

"She will not harm you."

To cover his embarrassment, Eddy said loudly, "I know how to ride. I exercise the ponies."

"You ever loved horses." Richard sounded distracted.

"You always say that! I mean . . . how do you know?" Abruptly he changed his tack. "She's so small. How could she kill anything?"

"Would you see her hunt?" There was a note of warning in the level voice.

Eddy ignored it. He would not show fear. Not ever again. "Yes!" Then under the speculative stare, he added, "That's what you brought her for, isn't it?"

For answer, Richard spurred his horse into a gallop. Gaffer followed, as fast as his shorter legs would allow. From behind Richard and his mount seemed one, carved from a single block of wood.

Richard reined in suddenly, pointing. A pigeon fluttered overhead. Richard's arm rose in a casting motion, and Jezebel was airborne.

The pigeon climbed frantically, but Jezebel closed the gap, wings rowing the air. Almost upon her quarry she seemed to check in midflight, then hurled herself upward until she was directly above it.

"She had it!" Eddy cried, shaking with excitement. "She almost had it. Why'd she stop?"

"She must kill from above. By speed and talon. It is the way of the falcon."

"Will she catch it now?"

"The pigeon has a trick or two left. See how it makes for yonder trees. If it gains shelter it may yet live another day."

Now the pigeon was climbing once more, dodging and twisting to elude the killing strike. But Jezebel pursued relentlessly, matching turn for turn, height for height. Huntress and hunted were almost at the trees now.

Eddy held his breath. Torn between thrill and pity, he longed for the pigeon to escape. Even as he lusted for the kill. His throat tightened.

With a last burst of speed, the pigeon gained sanctuary and was lost among the branches. Screaming her rage and frustration, Jezebel rose and swooped away in search of other prey.

"Quick, lad!" Richard shouted. "We must follow or lose her."

Eddy had boasted of his riding. But that dead run taught him he was still a rank beginner. He soon gave up all pretense at control and merely held on. Every muscle protested; his backside was so sore he groaned at each step. The skin along the insides of his legs chafed raw through his jeans.

They reached the top of a steep hill. He drew a breath of relief. Now they would have to slow down. Colin said you never ran the horses downhill. Richard would not risk the gray.

But to his horror, the pace did not slacken. Richard set his horse at the slope and bolted down. Gaffer followed gamely, but he was tiring. Halfway down he stumbled to his knees.

Eddy hurtled over his head, landing with a thud that drove the breath out of him. He lay gasping like a beached fish in an enormous silence.

At last he blinked, wriggled his arms and legs experimentally and sat up. Instantly the sky spun. The motion turned him sick, and he closed his eyes and lay back again.

There was a scrunch of hooves, then booted feet laboring over loose shale. Richard said roughly, "Are you hurt, lad?"

Cautiously Eddy opened one eye, then the other. The world had steadied. "I'm okay, I think."

"Thank God!"

He got to his feet and stood swaying slightly. "Gaffer?"

"The horse is unhurt."

"And Jezebel?"

Richard pointed. Gaffer grazed peacefully under a stand of trees. Jezebel perched on a branch overhead, surveying the world with her unblinking stare.

Bruised, sick and dizzy Eddy limped over to the pony. Blood seeped from a gash on his knee; he could feel it trickling down his leg. He stroked Gaffer's neck, whispering: "It's okay. It wasn't your fault."

Conscious of Richard's anxious stare, he growled: "What're we waiting for? Let's go.

It took all his willpower not to cry out as he hauled himself back into the saddle. Gaffer set off, picking his way with care. He seemed to know each step brought nausea and pain to his rider.

Eddy's mind was dazed and empty. But slowly he became aware of bird song, a tumble of clear notes cascading from above. He looked up to see a small brown bird skim past.

Richard followed his look. "A skylark," he said softly. "Her music is as fine as any lute or viol."

The whole world seemed focused on the piercing sweetness. Then it splintered. Jezebel screamed once before she hurtled from the branch as if shot from a sling.

It was over in seconds. The lark fluttered; Jezebel exploded onto it with the force of a dive-bomber. There was a sharp *thwack* as she hit. A puff of feathers. Then silence.

Eddy flung himself off Gaffer's back and ran toward the falcon, shouting: "No, Jezebel! No."

Richard's voice checked him. "Get back, Edward. The

lark is dead. You cannot save her. And Jezebel will hurt you if you try to take her kill. I will call her off."

Again he produced the dummy bird and swung it. Soon Jezebel was reseated on his wrist, obedience rewarded by a bit of meat from the pouch.

Eddy fell to his knees beside the dead lark. The impact of the strike had torn it to bits. The head was there, eyes open but dulling. Part of the breast still edged with bloody flesh. A scatter of feathers.

In an agony of pity and remorse, he picked up the remains, cradling them in his hands. Richard came to stand beside him and he thrust them at him. "Here! Feed them to your damned hawk. That's what you wanted, isn't it?"

Gently Richard put out a finger to touch the little head. On his other wrist, Jezebel tore at her meal, oblivious to her former prey. The sight of that cruel beak stuffed with carrion sickened Eddy. He fought back nausea.

Richard said softly, "The world is full of violence, Edward. The lark's song passes all too swiftly. We must give thanks for it while it yet lives."

"You don't care! It's just one more death to you."

"You willed it. You wished to see her hunt. Look, then. Look and remember. The falcon is as God made her. She kills to live."

"But you didn't have to let her. Just because I said. You knew what it would be like. And you had food for her all the time." The falcon's eye caught his. It glowed amber. Like Richard's own.

He said wonderingly, "She's so small."

"Small?" Richard's voice was heavy with bitterness. "Think you one must be large to kill? When my brother

Edward was king, he had a gyrfalcon. The bird of emperors. I had Jezebel. A peregrine for a duke. Yet she filled my stockpot." He gestured at himself, adding softly, "Nor does the hawk answer to its master's size. Only to his will. I was thirteen when Edward became King. I forged myself into his sword of vengeance. Scourge to his enemies. None asked if I were great or small when they trembled before me."

Eddy sprang up. In rage and pain too sharp for caution, he cried out: "Yeah! You know all about that, don't you! You and your Jezebel. You both kill to live!"

Richard's face looked scraped, skin drawn so tight the skull beneath gleamed through. His eyes were sunken, empty sockets staring blindly into darkness. For one more moment he and Jezebel were plainly visible; then, from one breath to the next, they and the gray horse were gone.

The silence ached, as if a presence had been torn from the bright air. Leaving nothing but void.

Slowly Eddy turned away. But there was one more task, to bury the lark in living earth. Carefully, lest he let fall his burden, he dropped to his knees again. But when he looked down at his cupped hands, they were empty. The lark too had disappeared.

X

He must have knelt there for a long time staring blankly, until the ache in his knees became intolerable and the deepening light warned him he must hurry back before Colin raised the alarm.

Once in the saddle he could only slump, deadweight. Gaffer too was done. The little bay staggered drunkenly. But in the end, he brought them safe home, clip-clopping into the stableyard to stand, head drooping, flanks heaving as he waited for Eddy to dismount.

Mrs. Bolton rushed to him. Colin was close behind, laboring over the cobbles on his crutches. The relief on both their faces changed to dismay when they saw the dirt and blood encrusted on his clothes.

But all Mrs. Bolton said was, "Took a spill, I see. Never mind. Any rider worth his salt comes a'cropper now and then." No questions. No reproaches. He loved her for it.

He tried to smile. But when he got down he couldn't repress a gasp of pain. His cuts and bruises had stiffened, and his head felt full of cotton wool. There was a high-pitched whine in his ears.

The stableyard swung tipsily, exploding into showers of sparks. Before his eyes the faces of his friends hung like two grinning pumpkins, then receded to the size of pin-heads. He giggled.

A hand took his arm. He struck out, fighting wildly to free himself. Mrs. Bolton half steered, half supported him to the car. She pushed him onto the front seat.

"Put your head down between your knees."

He obeyed. The whine abated and the fog began to lift. The heaving ground steadied, and he sat up. There was barely time to lean out of the car before he was violently sick, retching till there was nothing left but an ache in his chest and a sour taste in his mouth. Trembling with weakness, he leaned back again, wiping his streaming eyes and nose on his sleeve.

"See here, Mrs. B." Colin's fingers probed Eddy's matted hair. "Feel this. It's a monstrous great lump. Must of landed on it." His voice was hoarse with worry. "Never should of let him go off by himself like that."

"Nonsense. Anyone can take a spill. Haven't you ever? I'll get him straight home. A hot bath, dinner and a night's sleep and he'll be right as rain. You'll see. Now, you'd better look after that pony or we'll have two invalids on our hands."

Eddy managed a weak grin. "Don't blame Gaffer. It was my fault. I should have known better than to run him downhill. You warned me. But I was chasing—" He stopped. "See you in the morning."

Mrs. Bolton shook her head. "You'll have to take it quietly for a day or so, or we'll have you in hospital with concussion. Besides, had you forgotten? Your people will be here tomorrow afternoon."

His heart plummeted. To his dismay, his eyes filled. He turned his head aside.

Colin's hand closed over his. "Never fear, lad. You'll come back. And we'll be waiting, Gaffer and me."

"Sure." He had to clear his throat. "Sure. Maybe next year." Trying to sound natural, he added, "Give Gaffer a good rubdown. We went a long way today." They would never know how far!

As they drove away he fixed his eyes on the road ahead. Telling himself it was to keep the dizziness from coming back. Not because he couldn't bear to watch for the last time as Colin and Gaffer disappeared into the stables.

They would not miss him. No matter what Colin said. Middleham was their home, not his. He was a tourist. A summer visitor. He didn't belong here. Was there anywhere in the world he did belong?

As if she read his mind, Mrs. Bolton said, "You'll be back, Edward. Colin meant it, and so do I. You've just to say the word."

He shook his head despairingly. "You don't understand. It's too expensive. My parents saved for years to come. And Kate'll be in college soon and—" He felt as if deep inside him something bled continually. His hand crept to the lump on his head, then down to explore his gashed leg. Though all the while he knew the wound was not to his body but his heart.

Once home, Mrs. Bolton hustled him into the bath. The heat was comforting but when he got out he was shivering in short sharp bursts like a wet dog.

"Put this on." Through the half-open door she handed him a bathrobe smelling strongly of mothballs.

"It was Ian's. I knew it would come in handy someday."

It was far too long. He stumbled over the hem as he made his way back to his room. He said resentfully, "He must have been a giant."

"He complained of the doorways in this house. But— I've told you that before, haven't I?" She smiled tremulously. "It's all right, Edward. Don't look so stricken. It was a very long time ago. It's only that now and then—" She took a deep breath. "Mostly they're here with me.

George and Ian, I mean. I suppose it's why I've never even considered selling and moving south. Though each year the winters seem longer and colder." She straightened her shoulders. "I don't know what's come over me! Nattering at you like this when you should be in bed. Climb under the covers and I'll see to supper."

He heard her quick step descending the stairs. Moments later a cheerful clatter rose from the kitchen.

The chills had stopped, and he reached for a book. But the whine in his ears was back, insistent as a dentist's drill. Through the open window he thought he saw a winged shape silhouetted against the evening clouds. Was it Jezebel's jesses he had heard?

Mrs. Bolton touched his shoulder. "Here. Soup and scrambled eggs. Eat it all up. I'll keep you company."

He was ravenous. But there was something—something she had said. He stammered: "Before . . . you told me they're here with you . . ."

She flushed. "I didn't exactly mean . . ."

He was not to be put off. "What I want to know is, were you talking about—ghosts?" He flung the last word at her. Defiantly. The next minute he would have given anything to take it back. It was so . . . incriminating.

She was silent for a long time. He felt his chest tighten. Was she never going to answer? Fearful his expression would give him away, he lowered his face and began to eat.

When she spoke at last, it startled him so he almost dropped the spoon.

"Do you believe in ghosts, Edward?"

He stared speechlessly at her.

"Because, you see, people mean such different things by the word. I was referring to memory, of course. Not ectoplasm got up in sheets and jumping out of dark corners. But the continued presence of people we've loved and lost. So they remain part of our lives as long as we ourselves live."

Deftly she reached up to skewer a stray strand of hair into its bun. "Having you in the house these past weeks has brought them back. Especially Ian. Did you know he learned to ride at the same stables? Worked for his lessons, as you do, because we couldn't afford it otherwise? That's why it's been so marvelous. Like having him back." She glanced at him and said gently, "That's not fair to you, though, is it? Because you're Edward. Not Ian. A fine young man in your own right."

Was that all there was to it? Just memory? But he said only, "What was he like? I know he was big when he grew up. But wasn't he ever small for his age? Like me?"

"Never. He was a big baby and a big boy and a big man. He came by it honestly. George and I were tall."

"So's my father. How come I'm not?"

"You take after your mother. Kate after your father. Does it matter so much? Ian couldn't have ridden Gaffer, you know. His feet would have dragged."

He said hesitantly, "Someone said to me the falcon doesn't care if its master is big or little. It obeys his will, not his size."

"Where on earth did you run across a falconer?"

"Oh, I guess I just heard it somewhere. Maybe in a book. And you yourself said Richard the Third was a great warrior. Even though he was small."

She smiled. "I see our local hero has cast his spell on you."

It came too close to the truth. "We saw the play," he reminded her.

"Oh, Shakespeare!" Her tone was dismissive. "Richard's more kindly remembered around here. Especially in Middleham." She was quiet for a moment, then added, "You know, country folk believe ghosts walk if they've died by violence."

"Yeah. The guide at Warwick Castle said so too."

"Umm. Well, then, perhaps Richard haunts this town. He certainly died by violence. Although maybe it's not the violence, but that we all haunt the places we've loved. Become part of their special atmosphere. I suppose that's what I meant when I said George and Ian are still in this house. And Middleham was Richard's favorite home."

"But I thought—"

"You know, I grew up here in Middleham. My mother died when I was born. Like George, my father was a country doctor. Too busy to have much time for me. Though he sometimes took me when he made rounds. In a horse-drawn buggy in all sorts of weather." She smiled reminiscently.

"Of course, when there was danger of contagion, or anything he thought I shouldn't see, he left me outside. One day what he thought would be a five-minute call turned out to be a premature labor. In the excitement, he forgot about me. When he came out again five or six hours later, I was fast asleep on the buggy seat, wrapped in my overcoat. Luckily the horse was used to waiting and hadn't budged."

"Weren't you mad?"

144

"I suppose so. But he saved that baby and its mother. That was what counted."

Suddenly he was ashamed. Glad she hadn't heard him complain about waiting for his father at the lab. Because John Newby's work was lifesaving too. And he had a warm car to wait in.

She patted his hand. "You must forgive an old lady for maundering on."

"You're not old!"

"Eighty-three next month."

"My dad's sixty-one. And Mom's fifty-five. It's funny. They seem much older than you do. At least, they fuss more."

She laughed. "That's because they're only middle-aged. By the time you get this old you realize it's not worth it. Fussing, that is. In any event, what I started to say before I got sidetracked was that until I went away to school, I was left to my own devices a good deal. So I amused myself. Playing with the village children and in the castle grounds. I came to feel I knew Richard. When I rode out on my pony, I imagined he rode with me. And when I saw a hawk or falcon, I pretended we'd ridden out together for a day's hunting. I was his squire, you see."

He stole a look at the window but the dark shape was gone. If it had ever been there.

"My fantasies were more real to me than life. And more exciting. You might say Richard was more real to me than my father. He spent more time with me. We used to have long conversations. He gave me advice." She smiled a little sadly. "Of course, when I went away to school other people, other interests took his place. Perhaps it was just the fancies of a lonely child raised on local legends. I suppose it was better I grew out of it. Yet sometimes I miss him still."

Silently he promised himself, *I won't forget. Not ever.* But all he said was, "That first day when I went to the castle it felt like I was in a time machine. I even had some weird idea Richard was there." He hurried on: "The castle is really something! All that stuff—the furniture and clothes and food. I guess they keep it that way so we can see what it was like. Kind of like Madame Tussaud's without the figures."

She looked blank. Then she chuckled. "What an imagination! I can see I've met my match. Unless it's that bump on the head. Which reminds me." She glanced at her watch. "Time for you to get some rest. You'd better put on something warm. It's supposed to turn cold tonight."

He said without thinking, "My green sweater's in the drawer."

She was rummaging before he could protest. He heard her draw breath sharply. "What's this?"

She turned to face him with the knight on horseback in her hand.

He felt an odd sense of inevitability. Of dead stop. He had been waiting for it. It was too good to be true. All of it. Her friendship. Everything. It would not last. How could it? Now she would know him for what he was. A thief. A coward. Unworthy to follow Ian's footsteps. Or the Richard of her childhood dreams.

Yet he fought back. He had to. He said, "I got it at the market. After you left."

Her fingers probed the treasure. "Ahh!" It was a long-drawn sigh of satisfaction.

146

"What?" Did she recognize it? Know it for stolen goods?

"Unless I miss my guess, you've got a real find here. But it must have cost the earth. They're so rare."

The response was automatic. By now he believed it himself. "The man let me have it cheap. Because it's broken."

Astonishingly her face cleared. "I suppose he was just a 'fly-by-nighter.' These days anyone can call himself a dealer. Though he doesn't know or care what he sells. What a stroke of luck! I must say, though, you should have shown it to me before."

She put it down and stepped back a pace to admire it. "Didn't I say there were treasures to be found? I'm sure this is an authentic piece of Ripon work."

"Ripon work?"

"Yes. In the fourteenth and fifteenth centuries, Ripon was famous for its woodcarvers guild."

He felt deflated. Another antique. Something for his mother to gloat over. He lay back, sighing.

"I know. You must be exhausted. Delayed shock, most likely. I'll let you get some sleep." She brightened. "In the morning, if you're better, we'll go into York. I'll show you round the cathedral and we can take the statue to a friend of mine. He's curator of a small museum. If anyone can identify it he can."

Would a curator have heard of the theft? Did they send word to museums, like those wanted posters in post offices?

She fussed uncharacteristically, closing the window, pulling the blankets up to his chin until he felt like a mummy. For an instant he thought she was going to kiss him good-night. But she only patted him awkwardly and hurried from the room.

He was wakeful. The shock of discovery had lessened; miraculously he was still safe. Yet he hurt. Not just from the bump on the head, but with that same sense of impending loss he'd felt driving away from the stables. Only now he knew it was not just losing Colin or Gaffer or even Mrs. Bolton that he dreaded. He couldn't bear to lose Richard, either. Friends, all of them. Friends with whom—for the first time—he knew himself the person he longed to be.

By the time they reached York the next day, he was edgy with suspense. What would the statue reveal? Maddeningly, Mrs. Bolton seemed to have lost all sense of urgency. She lingered over each and every statue, plaque and tomb in the great cathedral. Before each piece of stained glass she delivered a lecture. At last she dragged him down to the crypt to see the Roman ruins uncovered there.

Museums and churches. He couldn't seem to get away from them. Two hours passed before he could remind her of their mission.

After that she set off willingly enough. He had to trot to keep up with her. Finally she drew him into a doorway. The hall inside was unlit but a cracked voice hailed them from the landing above: "Claudia! Claudia Bolton, where have you dropped from?"

"From Middleham, of course, Mr. Jonathan. I've brought a friend."

On the second floor a gnomelike figure met them. Eddy swallowed a grin as he looked at him. About a crumpled pink face, cottony hair stood out in disarray. Looks like he put a finger in a socket, Eddy thought.

But amusement changed to exasperation as their host refused to hear of their errand before serving tea. And as the old man fumbled for cups and searched crammed drawers for the biscuit tin, his impatience grew. Long before the kettle boiled on the gas ring, Eddy's temper was simmering.

"One lump of sugar or two?"

"What? Oh, two, I guess."

"That's right. That's right. Young people love their sweets." His smile was so infectious Eddy was suddenly ashamed of his bad temper.

He did his best to sip and listen politely as his companions discussed the archaeological finds under the cathedral. Just as he was wondering how he could contain himself longer, Mr. Jonathan reached for the package.

"What have we here?" His arthritic fingers made slow work of the knots. Eddy gritted his teeth.

Even Mrs. Bolton's patience had worn thin. She fidgeted, bursting out at last: "Oh, for pity's sake give it to me, Mr. Jonathan." And well before he had completed his examination, she prompted: "Well?"

"Oh, it's the real thing. Without a doubt. Ripon work, as you've probably guessed. Fifteenth century or thereabouts, I shouldn't wonder." He stroked the little figure lovingly. "A toy, of course. For a gentleman's son."

Eddy could not keep silent. "How do you know?"

"It's much too fine to have belonged to a commoner. Such things were costly."

"No. I meant, how do you know it was a toy?"

"Why, people didn't go in for what we call bric-a-brac

in those times. Especially here in the North Country, which was never so rich or sophisticated as London. No, this was a toy. Not an ornament. A toy with a purpose. Have you never played with toy soldiers?"

Eddy flushed. "My mom won't let me," he mumbled. "She hates war games."

"Pity. In those days a nobleman's son, even a knight's son, might have owned several of these. A small army to play at war with before he was set to real tilting and swordsmanship. Long before he led his own knights into battle, he had the rudiments of strategy."

Only a toy. An old toy. A child's plaything. No more important than a ball. Or the cars and trucks he'd loved. Or a teddy bear.

Yet could a toy have brought real battles to life—the thunder of horses charging, the whine of arrows, the screams of dying men? Would Richard have followed him from London for a toy?

"Are you sure?"

The old man looked offended. "I can't prove it, of course. But in my best judgment . . ." He looked narrowly at Eddy. "You seem disappointed. Would you consider selling? To the museum, of course."

Leave it here to gather dust on crowded shelves? He shook his head. Toy or not, it was his!

"Pity. A most unusual souvenir. Might I ask what you paid for it?"

Mrs. Bolton cut in. "Come, Mr. Jonathan, we're grateful. As you say, you've confirmed my guess. But you mustn't take advantage of my young friend. Now, I'm dying to see anything new in your collection."

Eddy followed, paying scant attention to the display of

Roman and medieval artifacts. If only he could tell them. The knight on horseback might be no more than a toy, but a ghost had recognized it. The ghost of Richard the Third!

The dusty rooms were airless and his head was aching again. Claudia Bolton looked at him and frowned. "You're white as a sheet. I'd better take you home."

For a moment, saying good-bye, Mr. Jonathan reminded Eddy of a child whose parents are going out. The old man waved forlornly as they walked away up the street.

Rain was falling as they drove out of the city. The windshield wipers clicked hypnotically—*click-swish* . . . *click-swish* . . . what child . . . what child . . . what child?

His head jerked up. What child? Until then it hadn't occurred to him to wonder. But if Mr. Jonathan were right, his statue had belonged to a child. What child? Was this the clue he had waited for?

The murdered princes! Had they taken it into the Tower with them? Played with it? Slept clutching it—the one familiar object in a threatening world?

Was that why Richard had pursued him? To erase a clue that might connect him with his victims? But how? And why hadn't he taken and destroyed it?

He felt Mrs. Bolton turn and look at him. "Asleep?"

"'Course not! I was just thinking." He peered out of the window. "This isn't the way we came."

"Sharp-eyed Eddy! You're right. It's a different road. There's something I want to show you. If you're feeling all right."

"I'm okay," he said curtly. "What is it?"

"A church. At Sheriff Hutton."

"What's so special about it?"

"Only that it's another fragment in the puzzle of Richard. You've seen the Tower. Tussaud's. Shakespeare's play. Bosworth and Middleham, of course. But this . . ."

He stared at her, challenging her to speak out. "Do you think he was a murderer?"

"It doesn't matter what I think. Or even what the truth was. What matters about Richard, about anyone, is what lies behind the facts. What kind of person he was. His whole life. That's what we must try to understand. Did you know that after Bosworth the city chroniclers of York wrote 'This day was our good King Richard piteously slain and murdered to the great heaviness of this city'? That's what his fellow North Countrymen—people he had ruled for years before he became king—thought of him. Whatever the truth of the princes' fate, that's also a fact to be weighed in the balance."

"Mom says there's no proof he killed them. But Dad says he put them in the Tower and they disappeared and he got to be king. It seems to me—"

"Your father's a scientist, isn't he? And scientists are taught to deal with facts. But there are all kinds of facts. Some can't be seen or touched or measured. Facts of the heart."

"Are you trying to say he was innocent? That he didn't kill them?"

"I'm only trying to say that people are complex. And their reasons can't be examined under a microscope. If Richard killed those boys, it was under dreadful pressure. Pressure for survival."

"But they were kids. They couldn't have hurt him."

"You have a lot to learn about politics. Especially the

cutthroat politics of Richard's day. If he had let either boy succeed to the throne, the courtiers around them—men who had envied Richard his brother's favor—would have destroyed him. And his family with him."

"That's no excuse for killing two kids."

"No. But it makes it more understandable. Perhaps less monstrous. Tragic, even. Think, Edward. What an awful choice to be faced with. Between his brother's sons, and safety for himself and his family. It can't have been easy for him."

He himself had stolen in blind panic. He hadn't meant to, but he had. Did that make him a thief? Two boys had disappeared and Richard had become king. Had he been their murderer?

Mrs. Bolton braked suddenly and pulled the car over to the roadside. They got out and she led him through a cattleguard and up a narrow path to a small gray church. In the rain it looked lonely and dejected.

Inside it was cold; there was an overpowering smell of damp. Shivering, Eddy followed Mrs. Bolton up the aisle to stand before a stone sarcophagus. The alabaster figure of a boy rested on the lid. His eyes were closed, his hands piously folded on his breast. The face was peaceful, even pathetic in its long sleep.

A wave of sadness came over Eddy. He bent to read the name, but the letters blurred. Who was the dead boy? What child?

He looked up at Mrs. Bolton and was startled to see tears on her cheeks. She fumbled for a handkerchief.

"Sorry," she said shakily, "but this place always affects me. It's the tomb of Richard's only son, who died at Middleham in 1484, at the age of eleven or twelve.

Richard and his wife were away at the time. The news reached them in Nottingham where they were holding court. Afterward Richard always spoke of Nottingham as the 'Castle of My Care.'" She took off her glasses and wiped them.

We shall not meet in Nottingham. No wonder he hadn't wanted to go back. Not even after five hundred years.

"They traveled north again, frantic with grief. At York Anne fell ill and could go no further. Richard went on to Middleham alone, to arrange for the funeral. He brought his son here for burial."

"Why not at Middleham?"

"No one knows. But I've always thought it was because he loved Middleham so. He had spent the happiest years of his life there. Perhaps he wanted to remember it that way. To keep one place free from sorrow. As a refuge. Poor man! For him there was to be no respite. His wife never recovered from the boy's death and died soon after. And in August of 1485 came Bosworth." Her voice trailed off. She blew her nose.

He knew she was thinking of her own husband and son, dead in a later war. He put his arm through hers and squeezed. Whether to comfort her or himself he wasn't sure.

She smiled down at him. "His name was Edward. I suppose that's why I brought you. It seemed only right for you to know. And remember."

154

XI

Behind them the church door opened. There was a rush of air bearing the pungent hint of coal smoke. Then the sound of booted footfalls on the stone flags.

Eddy retreated, pulling Mrs. Bolton with him into the shadows of a pillar. He didn't want her to be seen like this, the tears still streaking her worn cheeks.

"Let's go."

She resisted. "We've plenty of time."

Brilliance pierced the gloom. Turning, Eddy was blinded for a moment; gradually he made out figures moving through the church. The light flared from the leader's torch. Four men followed, bearing a small coffin on their shoulders. The sheen of raindrops on their cloaks was clearly visible as they passed; their faces were shrouded deep in their hoods.

He tugged at Mrs. Bolton's arm. "We can't stay here. There's going to be a service."

"Service? Oh, no. Not till Evensong and that's much later. About five-thirty. Besides, everyone is welcome."

He started to protest and thought better of it. Why not stay? He was curious. He had never been to a funeral. Not even his grandfather's. His mother had said he was too young. At the time he had been furious, but secretly relieved. He wasn't sure he wanted to see the corpse. Or know what they did with it. Besides, he might have giggled. Like when someone cried. He hated to see grown-ups cry. It terrified him. They weren't supposed to. They were grown-ups. So he had stayed home with the baby-sitter and pretended he didn't know what was happening.

Since then the forbidden rites had grown more and more intriguing. Like X-rated movies. Sometimes when he was alone he imagined himself at the center of such a drama. *Poor boy . . . so brave . . . so young to be an orphan.*

The men reached the altar. They laid their burden down before it and waited, motionless as statues. Even the flame of the torch was still, spearing up into the dark between the rafters without a flicker.

Again the door opened, admitting a procession led by a priest bearing a silver crucifix. Behind walked two acolytes, then a small phalanx of black-clad knights. Their cloaks swung open as they walked to reveal the metallic gleam of armor. A solitary figure stumbled after them. He fell to his knees in front of the coffin, as if his legs would no longer support him. His hood slipped back. His face was chalky in the torchlight, a death's head drowned in tears.

His cry shattered the silence: "Edward! Edward!" The harsh voice broke. His hands groped, clawing at the coffin as if to wrest the corpse inside back to life.

The sobbing went on and on. Eddy could bear it no longer. He covered his ears.

"Does your head ache?"

Didn't she see or hear it? Was she blind? And deaf?

"We'll go home. I'm afraid I shouldn't have let you out of bed today. Come along."

He was only too grateful to have her lead him away. He had seen too much death now—the terror of the princes in the Tower, Richard's own on Bosworth field, George and Ian Bolton's in the same war his father had fought in. Now there was Richard's son, dying with his parents faraway. Had he missed them? Cried for them at the last? If they had been with him, would he have lived? Could their love have saved him?

He clutched the statue as they drove away. Its very solidity was comforting. A hard fact. Something to hold onto.

Mr. Jonathan had called it a toy. That too was a fact. Until now Eddy had assumed it had belonged to the lost princes. Now it seemed there had been another child. Richard's own son Edward, whose funeral he had just seen. As if it lived on in the little church. As if five hundred years were not enough to erase the memory of pain.

The statue had been his! He was as sure of it as of his own name. Edward. The name they shared. Because Richard's ghost had been drawn to it unerringly. Was it the statue, or was it the name?

He leaned forward, as if his urgency could speed the car. He was suddenly impatient to get back. To Middleham where Richard had been happy. Where his own namesake had lived out his short life. There was something he had to do there. He was not sure what it was. He only knew that it had prodded him to Middleham from the first. Since he had found the statue and met Richard.

When they opened the door the phone was ringing. Mrs. Bolton ran to answer, calling over her shoulder: "Heavens, that must be your parents! I'm glad we didn't miss their call."

His heart sank. Soon they would be here and it would be over. He knew he should pack. Instead, he wandered into the living room and stood irresolutely, looking about. As though seeing it for the first time—the fat chairs in their chintzes, the threadbare oriental rugs, the family pictures marching across the mantel.

When Mrs. Bolton came back he started to say, "When will they be here?" But the words died because she looked so strange. Stricken. As if bracing herself for something she didn't want to do. Or say. Suddenly he was afraid.

"Edward." She stopped to clear her throat. "That was your mother. She . . . ah . . . asked me to explain they won't be here today. Your father is ill."

"You mean sick?"

"He developed chest pains after lunch. They've put him in hospital for tests and observation. In Durham. Now, you're not to worry too much. It's probably only indigestion."

What was it Kate had said? That the doctor had told John Newby he was the "type" for heart attacks? If so the warning had come too late. It had not protected him. No one could protect anyone. Even Richard with all his energy and courage had not been able to save his wife and child. Or even himself!

"He's dead, isn't he!" he said accusingly.

"I've just told you. They're running tests. Watching him. Purely precautionary."

"How come she didn't tell me herself?"

"She was upset. I suppose she was afraid that would upset you."

"I want to talk to her."

She put her arm around him. He shook it off and she retreated, flushing. "Look, Edward. I know how you feel. But getting angry won't help. When your mother calms down I'm sure she'll speak to you herself. It's just that

158

right now . . . well, people don't think clearly in a crisis."

He said loudly, "I want to see my father!"

"Even if we went there, they wouldn't let you see him. He's not allowed visitors. That's quite usual when someone has a—"

"A heart attack," he finished for her.

"Listen, Edward! It's not certain he's had one. They'll know better in a few hours. Meanwhile we just have to carry on. Your mother will ring back as soon as she can. With better news, I'm sure. Until then you must try to be brave and patient. Now, we'll both feel better when we've had our tea." She hurried out as though eager to get away.

He stared after her hopelessly. He had driven away his best friend. Just when he most needed her.

Presently, when he was sure the clatter of dishes and whistle of the kettle would cover the sounds, he tiptoed through the hall and went outside.

Windows in the houses as he passed seemed to stare accusingly. He bent low, trying to make himself inconspicuous. At first he walked slowly. Then faster. Soon he was running. Running to escape the tidal wave of panic that threatened to engulf him, sucking the air from his lungs, the blood from his veins. Running to the only refuge left, to the voice that called ever more insistently: *Edward, Edward when will you come home?*

Half-frightened, half-expectant, he came into the castle courtyard. As he looked around, his heart sank. It was empty, the turf smooth and unmarked by prints. Yet above the keep, a banner strained and flapped in the wind; he had last seen it in the great hall. Was it a welcome?

Heart beating faster, he climbed the steps and went into the keep. The hall was as before—a fire crackled on the hearth, the table on the dais was laid for a meal, weaponry hung ready on the walls. But it felt lifeless and untenanted. As if no one had been there for years.

At the far end the curtain across a doorway stirred. Was a watcher hidden there? He forced himself to go and yank the woolen folds aside. Beyond lay the passage he had walked with Richard. Today it was empty and dark; the torches were unlit. But a small light gleamed through the open chapel door. When he came there he found candles burning on the altar.

He slipped to his knees. "Please make him well. Don't let him die! Please." Not till he got back to his feet did the strangeness strike him. He never prayed. He wasn't even sure he believed in God. Yet here it had seemed natural. A part of his everyday life.

He could not face the dark corridor again; he opened a door on the other wall. To his relief it led outside. For a moment he just stood there, sucking in great gulps of air and feeling reprieved—from what, he didn't know. A short flight of steps at his feet led back to the courtyard. Slowly he descended. The certainty was growing. There was nothing here for him. Nothing for him to do but go back to face Mrs. Bolton's anger and the loss of her friendship. Back to face whatever was to be faced.

Yet as he crossed the drawbridge, he had to look back. Hopelessly. With no more than the confused need to carry the image of the castle away with him. A talisman against disaster.

What he saw there set his heart to pounding. High on the battlement stood a man. He waved. Unhesitatingly,

Eddy turned and went back. To Richard's world. To Richard.

As he toiled up the steps to the battlement he half-convinced himself it had been only an illusion. A mirage. Because he so dreaded yet so needed it to be true. Because if John Newby . . . then there was no one left for him. No one but Richard.

But when he came out onto the battlement Richard was waiting. Triumphant as Jezebel poised for the kill.

He said, "You have brought it!"

"Brought what?" Eddy said stupidly.

"The knight on horseback."

He had forgotten. But when he looked down he found to his surprise that he was carrying it. Clutched in his hands like an offering.

"You have brought it home!"

Suddenly he understood. "You meant me to. From the first. You never wanted it yourself. You meant me to bring it here."

"Yes."

There seemed nothing more to say. Together they leaned on the parapet looking down on the world below. From one side of the battlement they could see the village, a cluster of doll's houses. From the other the wall dropped sheer to the courtyard, a dream enclosed in stone.

I'm looking into two worlds, Eddy marveled. Two worlds five hundred years apart. From another place, another time his father's words came to him: *Someday, perhaps the universe will collapse into a black hole . . . a wormhole into another universe.* He himself was poised between those worlds. Which way should he turn? Could he ever get back?

Richard spoke in his ear: "We must be on our way." Then he said to someone else, though Eddy saw no one, "Are the horses ready? Good. We will be down directly."

"What do you mean? Where are we going?"

As if he hadn't heard, Richard only repeated, "We must be on our way. We have far to ride this night."

Eddy stammered: "But where . . . how . . . my horse isn't here."

Richard smiled. "Excited, lad? So you should be. I well remember my first encounter with the raiders." He made for the stairs, saying over his shoulder, "Hurry, lad. We must be miles from here by first light if we are to catch them."

He had no choice but to obey. When they reached the courtyard he stared incredulously. Tied to the hitching post at the stable door were two horses. The larger was Richard's gray. The other—could it be Gaffer?

The little horse nickered a welcome. Slowly, almost reluctantly, he moved to its side. It rubbed its nose against him, nuzzling at his pockets. "Gaffer?" he whispered.

Richard was in the saddle. Now he leaned down. "Come, Edward. It is almost daybreak."

Daybreak? It had been late afternoon when he left Mrs. Bolton's. How long had he been here? What time was it anyway? He glanced at his watch. Then changing his mind he took it off and put it in his pocket. It was of no use now. Because if John Newby—this time he completed the thought—if John Newby died, then nothing would ever be the same. Not even time. There would be no more time. Not as he had known it.

He packed the statue away in his saddlebag and swung

hastily into the saddle. As they clattered over the draw-bridge the moon appeared from behind drifting clouds. The village streets were dark and empty; no one and nothing to mark their going.

Yet as they came onto the moor Eddy was suddenly aware that others rode with them. He could not see or hear them, but he felt them around him, pressing close. There was the thrill of shared danger, a comradeship too deep to be denied.

And later—much later—as he swayed in the saddle half-drowned in sleep, his pony stumbled. Someone—not Richard, because he rode before—jerked the reins to keep the pony's head up. A voice spoke, or rather sounded, in Eddy's mind, saying, *Keep awake, lad*. Others laughed. Kindly laughter, not meant to shame. Richard must have heard because he looked back, smiling his thanks.

The night wore on. Still they rode, the long miles unrolling in a carpet of heather and brush and scree. At last Richard signaled a halt. Somehow Eddy slipped from the saddle. He would have fallen but something, someone caught him. Then he sank down into the grass and slept.

When he woke he was wrapped in a cloak but soaked with dew. Light was pouring over him; he blinked owlishly. The sky was so intensely blue it looked purple. On all sides the moor stretched empty, marked only by the few trees standing black against the luminous green of the grass.

Richard stood motionless and watchful on a knoll nearby. When Eddy stirred, he turned to him. "Good, you are awake. You must eat and then we will be on our way again."

He held out rough bread, cheese, a horn mug brimming with beer. Eddy reached out, then, remembering the piercing cold of that touch, drew back. Richard smiled and set the provisions down. He ate ravenously.

At a low whistle from Richard the horses trotted up.

"Where are the others?" Eddy asked.

"They have gone ahead to scout. We will catch them, never fear."

Richard was silent as they rode off, seemingly abstracted. After a time Eddy dared to ask: "Where are we going? Can't you tell me?"

"I had word yesterday. The Scots are over the borders again. Pillaging. Burning. Already they have burnt Bamburgh. We ride to cut them off as they move south. We shall teach them a lesson they will not soon forget."

Pillaging? Burning? Eddy stared. Had he forgotten? Scotland was at peace. Eddy's family was there. He shivered suddenly, as if a cloud had passed before the sun's face.

If Richard noticed he gave no sign. He kicked up his horse to a gallop, motioning for Eddy to follow.

Hours passed. It was the pony that told Eddy the unseen escort was with them again. It laid back its ears and kicked out at the unseen presences crowding up behind. Eddy almost cried out: *Hey! Don't get so close. Gaffer hates that.* Just in time he caught himself and kept silent.

As the hours passed the light changed imperceptibly. Every now and then Eddy reached for his watch. Only to let his hand fall to the reins again. Strange not to know the time. Strange yet somehow natural.

At last Richard called another halt. This time he set Eddy to scouring the ground for twigs and dried turf and they soon had a fire. From his saddlebags Richard produced meat, skewering it on his dagger to offer to the flames. It sizzled and spat, but when Eddy bit into it he found it barely cooked. Yet he wolfed down chunk after chunk, paying no attention to the bloody juices that dripped from his chin. There were apples too, bruised from their rough passage but still sweet. Replete at last he lay on his back in the grass and watched the clouds race by. A kestrel hovered, then winged lazily south.

From somewhere far off he could hear Richard and the others talking. At least it felt like hearing, though it was soundless and he could not make out what they said. Even as he struggled to understand, his eyelids closed and he slept again.

It was dark when he woke. The fire had guttered to embers. Richard was bending over him. Against the black sky he was huge and menacing, as he had been in nightmare. Eddy shrank back. Richard said only, "I'm sorry, Edward. I did not mean to startle you but we must ride on."

With the sun down the air was bitter; a sharp wind played across the lands. Eddy's muscles had stiffened as he slept. He thought longingly of Mrs. Bolton's house, his snug bed, his family. His family! For a time he had forgotten. For him there was no going back. Not ever!

He kicked his horse into a gallop, reining wide past Richard and the others. As he thundered past he thought he heard Richard cry out; the wind stole the sound away.

He bent low over the horse's neck, straining to see

165

through the darkness. But the drumming hoofbeats were hypnotic and after a time his attention wandered. He woke with a jerk from half-sleep and pulled up. The pony paid no attention. He pulled harder, but there was no stopping the racing animal. Its legs pumped faster and faster like runaway pistons.

Eddy's arms felt yanked from their sockets. "Whoa! Whoa, boy!" he gasped. The horse bolted on. Faster and faster. Eddy didn't dare turn and look back. But he cried imploringly: "Help! Richard, help!"

The land sloped sharply uphill and the horse redoubled its efforts. Breath labored through its nostrils in ragged gasps. Despairingly Eddy tried to work his feet out of the stirrups. If he threw himself sideways he might land in a soft spot.

His feet were free! He closed his eyes. Then he caught the thunder of hooves coming fast behind him. Moments later Richard's gray appeared beside him. Richard rode low, one hand clinging to the pommel, the other reaching out to grab for Eddy's reins. His hand closed on them and he jerked the speeding pony's head sideways. Suddenly the careening world was still.

Shaking with relief, Eddy could only cling there. Richard burst out: "In God's name, what were you thinking of? Running your horse like that in the dark! He might have tripped and broken your neck. You could have ridden into the raiders. Do you know what they would have done if they had caught you? Slain you without mercy! Worse, taken and held you for ransom had they known who you are."

Eddy couldn't meet his eyes. At last Richard said more

166

calmly, "No matter. You are safe. But we are closing on them and we must go quietly. Can you ride or shall I have one of the men lead you?"

"I'll ride," he muttered.

"Good." As they rode off he warned, "Remember, we must be careful from now on. No more running off. Though"—there was a chuckle in his voice—"I think you have little stomach left for such pranks."

Eddy was grateful that the darkness hid his crimson cheeks.

The ground grew rougher. They labored up steep inclines and picked their way down stony gullies. Once they splashed through a stream. The horses threw up sheets of icy water. By the time Eddy's horse stumbled up the far bank onto dry ground he was wet through.

The tension mounted. Now Richard stopped often to listen. The others would halt too, scarcely daring to breathe. Eddy's horse grew skittish, shying at shadows, dancing sideways when a rabbit ran across its path. At one point Richard's gray balked outright, refusing to pass a clump of gorse until Richard, cursing softly, got off and led him.

Eddy was silent. But the thoughts chased round and round his tired brain, like hamsters on a wire merry-go-round. He couldn't seem to turn them off. Would he have to fight? If so, how? He had no weapon. He wouldn't have known how to use it if he had.

Besides, the battle—or skirmish—was long past. He hadn't been there. How could he have? He hadn't lived yet. So how was it he was here now, riding with Richard and the others? What if he were wounded, even killed?

He put it aside finally, summoning up a will he hadn't known he possessed. He could only ride on. There was no other choice. He could not stay out on the moor alone, waiting for a raiding party Richard said would kill "without mercy." Or take him for ransom if they knew who he was. What had he meant by that? For an instant the glimmerings of an idea tugged at his brain. It was too fantastic and he pushed it away.

Ahead loomed a massive rock wall. In the cloud-haunted darkness, Eddy fancied for an instant it was a castle. Had they circled back to Middleham without his knowing? But as they came closer he saw it was a stony outcropping—a piece of the earth's spine thrust up in some ancient struggle.

Richard led them to the base of the rock and dismounted. About him, Eddy heard the chink of spurs and harness as the unseen company drew up.

Richard spoke softly: "We must leave the horses here. Go forward on foot. If I am right, we shall come upon the enemy yonder, beyond the cliffs." He turned to Eddy and a chill ran down the boy's back. Now, now he was to be tested. But Richard said, "Not you, Edward. I will not risk your life—" He broke off. Apparently thinking better of it, he went on: "Yet I cannot protect you always. You are old enough to know war. To see its cruelty." He pointed at the rocks. "From the top of the cliff you may watch safely."

Torn between relief, disappointment and a childlike desire to run after him pleading "Don't leave me here alone," Eddy could only watch silently as Richard strode away, followed—he knew—by the invisible band.

At last he crept to the rocks and looked up. Just then the moon appeared; its light fell full on the rock face. In the icy radiance rocks and clefts seemed like teeth, hungry to feast on his defenseless flesh. He shuddered.

Yet Richard had ordered him to watch. And Richard was all he had now. Gritting his teeth, he began to climb.

XII

Was it minutes or hours before he reached the top? He climbed blindly, not looking up or down, scrabbling for handholds in the scrub and rock. By the time he hauled himself over the last ledge to sprawl at the top of the cliff, he was sick and dizzy.

For a time he lay there with his eyes closed, gasping for breath. At last he lifted his head. Below, Richard's horse and his stood quietly. With them he knew—though he could not see them—were the other horses that had come the long way from Middleham. To the north stretched the moors—beyond sight, beyond imagination. He strained for a glimpse of the raiders. Or Richard. Of the raiders he saw nothing. And Richard might well have been swallowed by the night.

Panic clutched him. Would Richard come back? Or had he forgotten him? Did he mean him to find his own way back—as a test of his manhood and courage?

Then something—a mere pinpoint of light a mile or so away—caught his eye. He blinked and it flickered out, leaving the night darker than before. Even the moon was gone behind the clouds. But, no! The light was there again, a tiny spark that glittered like a diamond.

The spark blossomed, spreading until it was a conflagration. Now he could see it clearly. It was the light of a distant campfire. The flames leapt and fell only to rise again. Hypnotized, he stared at it. He could not look away. Now too he could make out moving shapes, patches of denser dark against the night's dark backdrop. As if something or someone crossed his line of vision.

He scrambled to his feet. Just above the horizon he saw a blaze of light—great flares of red and blue and yellow, burning and writhing like serpents in the sky. Were these the flames of raider's fires? Bamburgh and the other ravaged towns and castles? He thought of Coventry and his father's rage.

Suddenly he realized how exposed he was, silhouetted there against the sky. He dropped back to his knees. Even as he did, he saw something black and shapeless creeping stealthily along the cliff's base.

He held his breath. The thing resolved itself into a man crouched low. It straightened, beckoning to unseen followers; Eddy recognized Richard wrapped in his dark cloak. In his relief he almost called out, only to remember—in the nick of time—the need for silence.

He huddled there watching. Slowly it came to him the dark forms at the fire were raiders. They seemed unaware of their danger. Yet Richard and his men would soon be on them.

Unable to bear the suspense, he shut his eyes. But the scene was still there, a shadow play enacted in his mind. Richard, the invisible band, the raiders. Had he really seen them?

Even as he watched—or thought—Richard raised his arm. His sword flashed in the firelight. Other swords rose and fell. Hacking and cutting and stabbing. A confused clamor rose in Eddy's mind. It grew louder and louder. Shouts. Curses. Screams. A high-pitched yell. Was it the cry of a man in his last agony? Or only the wind, howling like a pack of hunting wolves?

He screwed his eyes tighter and put his hands over his ears. The images still rose and fell in his mind. The sounds of battle still reverberated in his ears.

A figure broke loose from the melee at the campfire. Momentarily it hesitated, seemingly uncertain which way to go. Then it turned and ran swiftly toward the cliff. Was it one of Richard's men, or a raider trying to escape?

Now there was a slithering at the base of the cliff, the rasp of a man's heavy breathing, then the scrunch of leather boots against rock. The man was climbing up! What would he do when he found Eddy?

Frozen with fear, he crouched there. But in his mind he whispered: *Richard! Come quickly. Please. Oh, please!*

A face materialized beside him. It was followed by an arm. Then with a grunt the man heaved himself up onto the ledge.

And at that moment another figure appeared. In a voice cracking with fury, a voice Eddy had never heard before, Richard cried out: "Would'st have at me through the boy? Coward! Coward!" The great sword rose and smashed down like a cleaver. There was a strangled moan, a bubbling sound, and a fountain of blood shot up, showering Eddy with sticky drops. The face disappeared, followed by the terrible sound of a body falling, bouncing from rock to rock.

Richard said anxiously, "You are not hurt?"

Eddy couldn't speak. He was staring at the sword in fascinated horror. The bloodstained blade was black in the moonlight. He managed to whisper: "Your sword. . ."

Richard looked at it with an expression of distaste. Wordlessly he unfastened his cloak and wiped the blade clean on it.

"It is finished. We must go home to Middleham."

Dawn was breaking as they rode off. The return seemed endless, yet timeless. After a while Eddy was no longer sure if it were day or night. Nor even if they moved at all or only rode in place, letting the winds flow over and around and under them in the illusion of motion. They rode and halted and rode and halted only to ride again. Rain followed the first dawn, and a bitter night the day.

Richard showed no discomfort, only wrapping his cloak more tightly around him. Eddy shuddered as he thought of the blood caked on it. But he said nothing. About him the unseen company was silent also. As if they had spent all reserves of speech and thought and feeling in the brief but deadly fight.

Not until they rode back into the castle courtyard did Eddy dare ask: "Will they come back? The raiders, I mean."

Richard climbed stiffly from his horse. In the moonlight his face was ghastly with fatigue. He said, "We left none to trouble us. There will be sore weeping in Scotland when the news is known. Yet more will follow. It is the way of the borders. He who would rule the North Country must be strong and swift to vengeance."

Eddy managed to get down without staggering. But when he retrieved the statue from the saddlebag, his hands shook with cold.

Richard was watching. His grim look changed to concern. "You are tired, Edward. Overtired. And your chest was ever delicate, like your mother's. I do not know what I was thinking of, taking you. Come. We will go to the nursery. There will be a fire there."

Eddy hung back. Suddenly he was nervous. Unsure.

Something more was expected of him. Something beyond the long ride and his witness to the campaign against the raiders. He didn't know what it was. He wasn't sure he wanted to.

"The horses! We've got to rub them down and—"

Richard smiled approval. "Good lad! It is the mark of a good knight to think first of his horse. But others will attend them. We must get you warm."

As he followed Richard through the courtyard his head was pounding. He wondered if he would be sick. Outside the mews he saw a hooded figure clinging to its perch. Jezebel?

They came at last to a small low-ceilinged room. A log fire was blazing in the fireplace. The room was warm and snug, furnished only with a chest, an oak bed, two stools, and a cradle pushed back into the corner. As if outgrown. Over the mantel hung a set of weapons. These were child-size, lethal toys.

Eddy stared longingly at them. Then he crossed the room and reached for the sword. As he did so he set the statue on the mantel. It looked at home, as if it had rested there before.

Richard drew the stools up to the fire and dropped onto one to sit with bent head, chin resting in his hands. He looked up inquiringly.

Eddy was hefting the sword. The hilt fit snugly in his grasp, as though made for him. He examined it more closely and found it engraved with a small army of knights on horseback. Like those he had ridden with.

He had been to battle and back. He had been blooded! Pride rose in him. For one breathless instant he imagined himself back on the moor. He raised the sword high, exulting in the sudden killing rage that coursed through him.

"Edward!"

The rebuke brought the blood to his cheeks. Not looking at Richard, he mumbled: "What?"

"Put the sword away!"

He dared not disobey. Sullenly he rehung the weapon, then hunched down on the other stool. Before sitting he took care to pull it further away, lest their knees touch accidentally.

"What do you want from me anyway?" he demanded. "I brought the statue back. And I went to fight the raiders with you and—" But he was ashamed. He had run to Richard in fear and grief. Richard had taken him in without question. Now . . .

Richard seemed stunned. "Want? Only to have you with me. Is it so strange for a man to want his own son?"

In the first calamitous shock it seemed to Eddy that if he kept still and pretended he had not heard, the words would go away. Disappear as if they had never been spoken.

Yet were they so shocking? Richard had known him from the first. That much was clear. He had known his name. He had recognized the statue. Over and over he had referred to memories—shared memories—of people, places, events. An entire shared life, in fact.

How long had Eddy known, known and been unwilling to face the knowledge? Had he first realized the incredible truth at the tomb in Sheriff Hutton? Or was it out on the moor when Richard had warned him of his fate at the hands of raiders?

Richard was on his feet now, knocking over the stool in

his agitation. He prowled the room restless as a caged animal. On the third pass he picked up the statue to stare hard at it.

Desperately Eddy racked his brains for something to say. Anything to turn the talk to other channels. "How do you think it got to the market in the first place?"

Richard frowned. "The statue? Nay, I know not. But"—he hesitated, then went on with suppressed violence—"I kept it ever by me after you . . . it was all I had left of you. So small a thing! It was in my gear at Bosworth. After that I do not know. Yet they laid bloody hands on all else that had been mine. Even the crown." He swallowed audibly. "I had meant to put it in your coffin. To light the lonely darkness for you, child that you were. You were ever fearful of the dark. Do you remember? Yet in the end I could not bring myself to part with it." For a moment he was quiet; then he smiled. "Do you remember the day Francis Lovell brought it for you from Ripon? How we played at war with it—the three of us?"

So Mr. Jonathan had been right! More right than he had dreamed. But he would never know. Because there would be no one to tell him. Eddy was not going back. Not ever!

Richard went on musingly: "Always—always I have wondered—if we had been there when you fell ill, instead of far away at court—"

Before the anguish in his eyes Eddy said the first thing that came to mind: "I guess the doctors weren't so hot in those days."

To his surprise, Richard laughed.

"What's funny?"

"I had forgotten. What folly to torment myself so! The

past is past. For us—for you and me—the future lies ahead. The fireside in winter when the wind blows sharp. The moor in summer with hawk and hound for sport. Lark song." He glanced at Eddy and hurried on. "No more illness. No more pain or war. Forever."

Against his will Eddy was caught up by the words. Once more he smelled the sweet grass, felt Gaffer's warmth between his thighs, knew the cobweb touch of mist on his face. Out of the depths of his own longing he whispered: "Oh, if I stay will you teach me to hawk and hunt? And to fight, really fight? Like back there on the moor? Not with toy soldiers but with weapons like the sword you used to save me. Like the one over the mantel. It was my sword, wasn't it?"

Richard shook his head. His face was grave. "Has there not been enough killing? Did you not see enough bloodshed at Bosworth and back there on the moor? Those were men, Edward. Even the enemy were—are—men."

"But you were a soldier. And you saved my life. Even if you were small and—" He bit off the next word. He had been about to say "crippled." But it wasn't true. He could see that now. "You told me you made yourself your brother's sword. You said the ruler of the North Country must be 'strong and swift to vengeance.' Remember?"

Richard leaned forward. He thrust both hands into Eddy's face; before their steely strength he drew back.

"Look, my Edward. Look well. These hands that never touched you save in tender love have wielded sword and battle ax. They have separated men's heads from their necks. You yourself have seen it. You know why. Yet it was not for entertainment, to please perfumed courtiers and their ladies. Nor yet to amuse an eager boy. Even my own son! It was only in combat. Deadly combat. I killed to live! As you yourself once said. Do you remember?"

He could only nod, still staring at those hands.

"Yet you still do not understand. How could you? Until we went to slay the raiders I protected you always. Perhaps too much. You do not know what it means to kill. To snuff out a life as easily as a candle flame. Not as Jezebel does—to eat—but to live. I killed only to live. That I and those I loved might live, not perish at our enemies' hands. And that my people might live in peace. For, as God is my witness, had I gained the victory at Bosworth, I should have passed the rest of my days in peaceful governance. For you, for myself, for England, I wished only peace!"

He said incredulously, "You mean you didn't like to fight? You'd rather just have signed papers, passed laws?"

"Before I became king, I ruled the north. My greatest joy was to bring good into men's lives. No plea was too small, no cause too humble to attend. I forced the great lords to cast down the fish garths that the poor might fish the streams, my meanest subject bring catch home to feed his children. All England would have smiled beneath my hand." He shrugged wearily. "Instead she groaned under the Tudor."

The fire was dying. One last tongue of flame licked feebly at the charred logs but the room was growing cold. The dark reclaimed its kingdom.

Abruptly Eddy stood up. "Let's go outside!" He had to move. Right now. To have time to think. Otherwise—

otherwise he would never tear himself away. Did he even want to?

The night wind struck their faces. Eddy thrust his hands deep in his pockets. He tried to whistle. But no sound came from his chilled lips.

There was a rush of wings overhead; black shapes swooped away into the darkness. Behind them trailed a long liquid whimpering: "Koo . . . oo . . . oo." Rising and falling, like the cry of a hound in pain.

Eddy cried out. Richard exclaimed and crossed himself. "Gabriel's Hounds!"

"What are they?" Eddy's voice shook.

"Country folk call them the harbingers of death."

Lights burned in the village below. Homely fireflies, lamps to hold back night terrors. Suddenly he longed to be there, safe with Claudia Bolton and the others. And then he remembered again. For him there was no safety there. Only emptiness. Safety was here with Richard. Yet . . .

For an instant, he almost wished the voice in his head would speak. It had been silent these past weeks. If only it would tell him what to do!

"Do not be afraid, my son. I spoke in haste. It was their cry that startled me. They are but birds—whimpernels. Their flight oft heralds storms. None but the unlettered think they bring death. And look you—for us, for you and me—there is no more death. Nought left to fear save loneliness. And that too is vanquished since we found each other again!"

Was it true? Could it be true that if he stayed he would live forever? Even though his father was dead?

179

"What—what makes you so sure I'm your son?"

Richard smiled. "Should a father not know his son's face? Into whose hand but yours would a just God have restored the knight on horseback? As he has returned you to me! If only your mother—"

His mother! He hadn't spared a thought for her since he had run out of Mrs. Bolton's house. Scared. Angry. Hurt because she hadn't told him herself.

He had a sudden vision of her face, blind and stupid with tears. Like Mrs. Bolton's at the tomb in Sheriff Hutton. Like Richard's own. Would she look like that when . . . if he saw her? Or would she try to hide it? Which would be worse?

But what of the other woman? Try as he would, he could not make her out. Yet she was there—somewhere—in the recesses of memory. If only he could see her! If only it weren't so dark. If he stayed here would he—

He said, "That room you showed me the other day. With the clothes and the perfume. The muddy boots . . ."

Richard's face blazed. "Yes, Anne's. My Anne. Your mother! The room is as she left it. If only she could see you as you are now. Still gentle and good, yet grown so big and strong!"

Was he really that way? Was that what he was like? "I wish—oh, I wish—" The words were dragged out of him. He bit them back, aghast. What was he saying?

Because he couldn't stay. He had to go back. He knew that now. If his father died they would need him, his mother and Kate. They would need him more than ever before.

Only that other woman . . . Anne . . . her perfume had been so sweet!

"I have to go!" He said it loudly. As if explaining to a child. He could not bring himself to look into Richard's eyes. "I don't want to. Not really. But—" It was the only crumb of comfort he could offer. And it was true. The castle, the horses, the North Country were part of his life now. Part of him. As Richard himself was! What would Eddy be without them? Who would he be? Who *was* Eddy Newby?

"If you did not mean to stay, then why did you come back?"

"You made me!" He shouted the words over the lump in his throat. "Can't you understand? You made me!"

Before his fury Richard stepped back. But he said only, "Weep not, my Edward."

"I'm not crying!"

"Because I see now it was folly, selfish folly, to hope to keep you. You did not die by violence; for you there may be rest. Come, you must not cry so. Rather, let us give thanks to the good God that he has granted us this time together. Here, where once we were happy." His voice shook on the last words.

Drawing his cloak about him he turned and walked swiftly away. He did not look back. But at the tower door he paused, raising one hand in brief salute.

"Farewell, my Edward. Rest well."

XIII

Long after Richard was gone Eddy thought he still could see him, burned against the dark as if by photo-flash. And long after his footsteps had died away, he heard them echoing and re-echoing along the battlement.

Now at last it was quiet. Too quiet. Even the ever-present moorland wind was still. The air hung limp and clammy. He could almost taste it, stretch out a hand and grasp it.

For a time he simply waited, listening to that unnatural silence, feeling the night press in on him. But in the end he roused himself. It was time, past time to start back. He had been gone—how long was it? Two days or three? Even the imperturbable Mrs. Bolton would be frantic. He didn't want to think about what his family must be feeling. And by now there was bound to be news of his father.

Yet he hardly seemed able to make the effort. Was it fatigue or the pain of losing Richard? He felt as heavy and inert as the air around him. Reluctant to go back. Afraid to find out what had happened. It was easier not to know, to pretend it had been a mistake, a nightmare from which he would soon wake up.

Oh, why hadn't he chosen to stay? Why had he sent Richard away? He was gone forever! They would not see each other again. One part of Eddy knew it. While the other refused to believe it—straining to see and hear him still. He found himself whispering over and over like an incantation: "Just once more. Please! Just one more time." Pleading to see Richard again. Pleading with him to come back. To save him as he had in the fog, and when his horse had bolted. And when the raider had come after him. Pleading—he didn't know for what. Pleading as if he were still there to hear.

The words dropped into silence.

He tried again. "I don't blame you for being mad. But I didn't know. I didn't understand. Please come back. Oh, please! I need you." He hardly knew if it were Richard or his father he pleaded with.

But in the end he had to face it. Richard was gone. As if he had never existed. He was gone and Eddy was alone.

As yet it hardly hurt. Pain would come later when blood seeped back into the shocked tissues of mind and heart. Right now he felt nothing. Except the tiredness and cold.

It was the cold that roused him finally. He had to move or freeze. If only it weren't so dark. He couldn't ever remember a night so dark. He brushed a hand across his eyes but now he could not even see the parapet. Or the lights in the village below.

The stone underfoot was rough; he stumbled as he groped his way forward. In his mind he rehearsed his path, thoughts running free before his faltering feet. Back along the battlement to the tower door. Then down the winding stair that passed the nursery where Richard and he had sat before the fire. How long ago had it been?

The steps would be treacherous. But there were torches. And he could stop and sit by the nursery fire for a little. Poke it up and warm his frozen hands. Retrieve the statue. Because with Richard gone there was no reason to leave it. No one here to whom it mattered. And it was all he had to remind him. Of Richard. And of who he himself might have been.

Yet would the fire drive out the cold that infiltrated his bones? Could a piece of carved wood fill the emptiness inside him?

"I have to go back. They need me now." The words forced past his trembling lips.

One step. Then another. Trying all the while to make out something—a glimmer of light or landmark. Shouldn't he have reached the tower? Had they come so far along the battlement?

He smiled suddenly. His father always said "Distances are deceptive in the dark." How Eddy loved his yarns! War stories about men who fought over ground for days, only to blunder like blind moths after nightfall. Well, he would have his own stories to tell when he got back. If he ever got back!

What had happened to the moon? He could swear it had been there, hanging like a great silver globe above the courtyard when they'd ridden in.

Suddenly something about the air—the clamminess, the tang of it—jogged his memory. How could he have forgotten his first day on the moor?

Sea fret! The sudden blinding fog that blew in from the sea, blanketing the land with terrifying speed. Of course!

Oddly the realization was steadying. He would find his way, fog or no fog. Hadn't Richard found him in the fog? Now *he* must find his way, for his mother's sake and Kate's. His father always said he had the best bump of direction in the family. Not like Kate, who'd been known to lose her way going to the john at night.

The tower must be just ahead. He frowned. He should have seen the torchlight by now, shining through the open door. Unless Richard had shut it. That was it; it had to be.

He felt for the door handle. As he did so something, some sixth sense or intuition, jerked him back as sharply as a restraining hand. For an instant he fancied he felt it and whirled, giddy with relief. It must be Richard. Come back for him after all.

Even as words of welcome rose to his lips, he heard the ominous rattle of loose stone sliding into an unseen chasm. Suddenly the air was filled with turbulence. A gust of wind clawed at him.

And as if a curtain parted the mist was gone. He could see again.

He blinked unbelievingly. Because the towers, walls and battlements that he had known were gone. Vanished as if a magician had waved his wand. In their place were only heaps of shattered rock, forbidding as an Arctic ice-field. And as tumbled, twisted and broken. No more than the skeleton of Richard's stronghold. Middleham Castle lay in ruins!

It was concussion. That was it. Somewhere he'd read concussion gave you double vision, blurriness. Maybe if he closed his eyes . . . He shut them and began to count, drawing it out. One . . . twooo . . . threeee . . . At one hundred his eyes flew open again.

The disappointment was shattering. Stark incredulity followed. What had happened? What could have caused such devastation? Had there been a nuclear war? But there had been no hint, no warning.

Or could it be Richard's revenge? Had he—like Samson—pulled the castle down about their ears because Eddy refused to stay?

Like a thunderbolt it came to him. He should have known. Mrs. Bolton's astonishment when he spoke of the castle and its furnishings should have told him! To the world, Middleham had been a ruin for years. Perhaps centuries!

Only for Richard was it still the refuge he had known and loved, perpetually the same, caught up in time out of time, a time warp, in fact. Into that illusory world—half-dream, half-real—Eddy had strayed, drawn by Richard's love and longing for his dead son. Rejecting it, he was forever barred from the magical precincts.

Now too he saw his danger. It turned him cold. He was a prisoner, marooned high above the world on a broken platform of stone that had once formed part of the battlement. It was no more than a fragment, perhaps six feet long by two feet wide. If he had stumbled off it in the fog. . . . He shivered. Because the parapet was gone. Nothing separated him from the fatal drop to courtyard or village.

The courtyard itself was a shell, a mere floor plan of the structures it had housed. Stables, mews, even the great keep was gone. Only fragments, truncated pillars, remained to mark where they had once stood.

The section of tower nearest to him was a gutted half shell now, open to wind and weather. One or two turns of staircase still clung to its inner surface. But they hung unsupported over emptiness. There was no way down!

He reached out a shaking hand to steady himself.

There was nothing to grasp! He inched back to dead center of the perch and huddled there, too terrified to move. The slightest breath dislodged another shower of loose rock.

Time passed and fear grew. His body prickled as if an army of insects were marching over him. He shuddered at the touch of those dry inhuman feet.

Was he to die here? Would his flesh rot, leaving the bones to shrivel into powder, forever blowing on the restless winds? Like the dead at Bosworth field? Like the Scottish raiders on the moor?

Dazed and exhausted he fell asleep at last, head pillowed in his arms. An uneasy dream-haunted sleep filled with pictures of Richard—Richard on horseback, cloak blowing out behind him; Richard's body slung across a pack horse, the horse stumbling as they came into Leicester so the dead skull cracked against a bridge abutment. Eddy winced at the sound and a murmur rose from the watching crowd.

The murmur swelled, resolving itself into voices. "Eddy? Where are you, Eddy?"

He raised his head. He was cramped and stiff; he groaned as he crawled to the edge and peered over. Then he caught his breath. There were lights now—lights coming toward him through the village streets!

"Eddy! Can you hear me? Where are you?"

He found his voice. "Here! I'm up here."

"Where?"

"On the wall. I can't get down."

The lights were on the drawbridge now. Momentarily the portcullis hid them; then they were in the courtyard itself. To his dazzled eyes, the torches and lanterns shone like a galaxy of stars.

"Eddy?"

It wasn't. It couldn't be John Newby!

"Eddy?"

It was. Oh, it was!

"I can see you now. Don't try to move. The rock's rotten. It might break away."

"Dad?" He still could hardly believe it.

"Yes. It's all right, son. Just don't move. We'll get to you."

It was the relief that undid him. He pleaded: "How long—how long will it take?"

"Colin's gone for tackle. He should be back any minute. We can't wait for daylight. They're predicting storms."

So Richard had been right. The whimpernels *had* heralded a storm. "If the rock's bad, then how will he . . ."

"Colin's an experienced climber. Is there anything up there to make fast a line?"

He felt about. "There's a sort of stump. From the old parapet, I guess."

To his relief he heard the throb of the Land Rover from the stables. It roared into the courtyard and jolted to a stop just below. He watched as willing hands unlashed the ladders from its roof and flung them up against the wall. A man emerged and started up, climbing steadily despite the heavy coil of rope slung over his shoulders. When he reached the top of the ladder he braced himself and stared up.

"Eddy?" It was Colin's voice. "You all right, lad?"

"Yeah. But am I glad to see you!"

"Listen. These ladders won't reach the whole way. I've got to come the rest by rope. I'm going to toss you the end. Make it fast."

"How?"

"Did you forget the knots I taught you?"

The line snaked through the air. He grabbed, missed, and watched helplessly as it slid back, accompanied by that ominous shower of stones.

Colin swore.

Three times more the rope sang. Twice it missed entirely; on the third try Eddy got a hand on it only to feel it slide away again.

"I can't!" He was close to tears.

"Steady, lad. I'm going back down for a grapple. Should've known I'd need it with the loose rock and the light so bad and all."

Eddy shut his eyes. Even so it seemed an eternity before he heard Colin shout: "Right, now. Watch yourself."

Miraculously it bit on the first throw. Eddy's hand closed over the line. He struggled to secure it on the stump of rock.

At last he called: "Okay!"

"Keep a hand on it where it goes over the edge to keep it from fraying."

He felt the line jerk as it took Colin's weight. But he held firm, guiding it safely from the knife-edge. He didn't dare watch as Colin, line about his waist, scrambled up the sheer wall. Despite the cold, sweat was pouring off him before Colin was beside him, grabbing his shoulders in a grip that made him wince.

"You gave us a proper fright, lad! We thought you'd run off on the moor—and the fog so thick neither man nor beast could move."

"How . . . how long was I gone?"

Colin laughed. "You mean you don't know? But then, I suppose in the fog it was hard to tell. Though I'd have thought your stomach would've told you. The way you eat! Still, Mrs. B. said the last she saw of you was about four yesterday afternoon. She was getting tea. Next thing she knew, you were gone." He made no mention of the reason for Eddy's flight. Maybe Mrs. Bolton hadn't told him.

"What time is it now?"

"Round about four in the morning. You've been gone close to twelve hours. Feels like more, I can tell you! I wouldn't want to be in your shoes when your folks get their hands on you. Or Mrs. B., for that matter." The prospect of a row seemed to please him.

Eddy was silent. Twelve hours. Yet for Eddy, for Richard and his company, several days had passed!

"Beats me how you got up here."

Hastily Eddy said, "What about Gaffer?"

"Gaffer? Oh, he got home hours ago. Wandered off when you climbed up. Got tired of waiting, I guess. Though how you . . ."

So the pony *had* been Gaffer! He might have known. Yet . . . "Your ankle. How could you climb with it? Last time I saw you"—he paused—"day before yesterday, I think, you were on crutches."

"Doc strapped it. After all, when a friend's in trouble—" He squeezed Eddy's shoulder again. Then, as if embarrassed at this show of feelings, he called down to the waiting crowd: "He's fine! I'm sending him down. Get set to steady the ladders when he reaches them."

Swiftly he untied the line from his waist and fastened it around Eddy.

"Climber's knots," he explained. "When I was a boy, I spent half my time on the cliffs hereabouts. Hunting falcons' nests. Till my father discovered I was skipping school. Caught bloody hell for it. Not to speak of falcons being an endangered species, so it's illegal."

Eddy suspected he was rattling on to distract him from the climb ahead.

"There!" Colin grunted with satisfaction as he secured the last hitch. "Over the edge with you. No, not that way. Face me and lean out against the rope. It'll hold. And I'll be on this end."

"I've never used a rope."

"It's either that or fly. Same way you must've come up."

He never knew if he mustered the courage to put the first leg over, or if Colin simply lifted him. But the next thing he knew he was dangling in midair, the rope taking his weight as his feet scrabbled for holds.

Above, he could see Colin's head silhouetted against the black sky. "That's right. Lean back. Right away from the wall. Now let your feet walk down. Good lad."

The rope felt as if it would cut him in half. He was breathless, whether from the rope or terror he didn't know. He was sure he hung there, paralyzed with fright, for hours. But slowly his feet began the descent. His hands clenched the rope in a death grip as Colin paid it out, inch by torturous inch.

Just once he looked down. Instantly the chasm beneath spun in dizzying patterns of black shot through with livid streaks. He froze, gulping back sickness.

"Don't look down!" The sharp command startled him into motion again.

Time was suspended—without beginning, without end. There was nothing in the whole world but the search for toeholds, the unending battle to force each foot from its safe niche and down again. As he stared up the sky lightened to mottled silver, painted over by blown cloud. Dreamily he recalled the night flight to England so many weeks before; they had floated over snowfields of cloud until dawn brought the descent to London.

At last his sneaker encountered an obstacle. A babble of voices broke out: "That's done it!" "Good lad." "The rest is easy."

"Untie yourself," Colin shouted. "I'll pull the line up for myself."

Mechanically he descended the ladder. Down . . . down . . . down . . . Then strong arms grabbed him, swinging him off the rungs into a bearlike embrace.

"Eddy!" John Newby's voice was choked. "Oh, Eddy!"

He butted his head into his father's chest and hung on as if he were drowning. Finally he managed to say, "I'm okay. But I thought—Mom phoned and said you—"

"I know. It was a real scare. Turned out to be mostly indigestion. I had some kind of meat pasty for lunch. Should have known better. It tasted like something left over from the Dark Ages! I guess I'm too old for that sort of thing." He looked down at Eddy and added softly,

"They tell me I've got a touch of angina too. Nothing to worry about so long as I take it easier. Keep pills by me. But I'll need your help. I haven't said anything to Kate. Or your mother. You know how they worry."

For a moment he couldn't speak. Then he said, "I promise, Dad. I won't say anything." He tried to laugh. "We'll be a walking pill supply, you and me."

His father stared at him. In the gray light his face was hard to read. At last he smiled. "You know, son, I think maybe we've both learned something these past weeks. I'd better take time to know you better. After all, you're the only son I've got. If there's one thing a scare like this teaches you, it's not to take things for granted."

A shout announced that Colin too had made a safe descent. He came to stand beside them. Without letting go of Eddy, Dr. Newby wrung his hand.

"That boy of yours!" Colin shook his head. "A ruddy mountain goat. I'll never fathom it."

"What matters is, he's safe. Thanks to you."

And to Richard, Eddy added silently. Aloud he said, "How was Scotland?"

"Scotland? Just fine. Why?"

"Was there any sort of trouble?"

"Of course not. Why should there be?"

"I dunno. Did you go past Bamburgh?"

"That's in England, not Scotland. On the northeast coast. We didn't get over there. Would you like to see it?"

"No. I mean, sure! It's just . . . I heard there was a fire there and—"

Colin laughed. "Someone's been putting you on! Bamburgh burned in 1482. Attacked by Scottish raiders.

Duke Richard led the Yorkshiremen against them."

And left them dead on the moor, Eddy thought. Soberly he disentangled himself.

The courtyard was alive with people. They had hung back, leaving him to his father. Now they crowded up, smiling and reaching out to touch him. His adventure had spelled trouble, even danger for all of them. For him they had gone out on a night of fog and cold. Yet he saw no reproach on their faces, only happiness at his safe return.

There was a commotion at the fringes of the crowd. Then Kate and Mrs. Newby broke through, followed closely by Claudia Bolton.

"D-darling!" His mother's cheek was wet against his. He hugged her, feeling as if he comforted a frightened child.

She held him at arm's length, saying, tremulously, "You've g-grown so b-big and healthy. In just two weeks. Wh-where's my little boy gone?"

Kate put her arms around him, saying, "Eddy! Oh, Eddy!" in a voice he'd never heard her use.

He turned a little shamefacedly to Mrs. Bolton.

"Well, Edward?"

"I'm sorry. Really sorry. I didn't mean to make trouble. I was scared. I guess I went a little crazy."

"I know." She smiled at the crowd. "There's no way. No way at all to thank you properly. But you must know how grateful we all are."

"Yes," Dr. Newby agreed. "You've given us back our son."

They dispersed slowly, men and equipment making their way back across the drawbridge and through the

194

sleeping streets. At last the castle grounds were silent, deserted except for Mrs. Bolton and the Newbys.

"Can I come back in the morning—before we leave?" said Eddy.

Kate stared at him. "I should think you'd never want to see it again!"

He did not answer. He was looking about, imprinting the scene on his memory. In the silvery light the crumbling stone seemed to shimmer. Like light refracted through deep waters.

"Beautiful, isn't it?" his father said softly.

He nodded, unwilling to spoil the magic with words.

"Come on! We can't moon around all night. I must say I agree with Kate. I never want to see or hear of Middleham Castle again." Mrs. Newby's voice was sharp with strain.

Mrs. Bolton put an arm around her. "Come, my dear. You've had a trying day. You'll feel better after a few hours of sleep."

Eddy hung back. "Please!" he insisted. "I want to come back before we leave. Just one more time." He ached. For the castle the others would never see. Most of all for Richard who had wanted nothing, asked nothing of him but that he exist.

"We'll see," said his father. "But right now we'd all better get some sleep."

It was then that he heard hoofbeats. They seemed to come from the open moor to the south. Crying "Wait for me" to the others, he began to run. When he reached the broken rear wall he hoisted himself up to look over.

The land stretched empty. Yet he could still hear

hooves. Then as he strained to penetrate the darkness, he thought he saw something. Was it no more than a shadow cast by the ragged clouds scudding across the moon? Or was it a horse and rider? It seemed to him it halted briefly at the crest of the hill behind the castle.

His heart lurched. Was it Richard come back for him after all? He twisted about to look over his shoulder and see if the others had noticed. But they still stood in a dispirited group under the portcullis. His father bent over his pipe; a match flared and died between his cupped palms.

Eddy turned back. Even as he did, the shadow disappeared over the hilltop and was lost from view. Gradually the hoofbeats grew softer until they could no longer be heard at all.

He rubbed his eyes. Had he seen Richard, or felt his presence as he had the horses at Bosworth and the invisible company riding with him after the raiders? Or was it only the longing of his own heart?

"Coming, son?"

Salt tears coursed down his cheeks. He gulped and snuffled. "Yeah, Dad. I'm coming."

As they came out into the square before the castle he looked back again. Just once. The clouds were thickening, but high up in the ruined tower he thought he spied a light. And for an instant he saw Richard clearly, sitting on the stool before the nursery fire. He was alone now, but the knight on horseback stood on the mantel. Edward's knight.

As if from far off he caught a faint jingle of harness, the weary scuffle of a horse's hooves as it shifted from foot to foot, waiting to be unsaddled. He made a move as if to go to it, then turned away again. Soon Richard would remember and come down to lead the big gray into the stables. There was no more Eddy could do. The horse was in Richard's world now. Not his.

He wondered if he would ever return. If so, he would neither see nor hear them again. Yet they would be here still—the statue, Jezebel, the horses, Richard and his men. The knowledge comforted him.

He dug his hand into his pocket and touched the fragment of sword he had carried with him since the day at Bosworth. Then he cried, "Hey, wait up!" and ran to join the others.

MIDDLEHAM

Spare ruin abandoned
to the famished winds,
skeleton built not of stone
but tears; a frozen breath,
a fossil in the sun, flesh
wasted, bones forgotten

while ghosts of harnessed horses
at the gate droop, waiting
for Plantagenet return.